QUARANTINE STREET LIT SERIES

the virus brought me my FIRST Love

4XS *NEW YORK TIMES* BEST-SELLING AUTHOR

WAHIDA CLARK PRESENTS

the virus brought me my FIRST Love

QUARANTINE STREET TALES SERIES

WAHIDA CLARK

All Rights Reserved. No part of this book may be reproduced or transmitted in any form by any means, electronic, photocopying, mechanical, recording, information storage or retrieval system without permission from the publisher. None of the material in this writing can be reproduced without written permission from Wahida Clark Presents Publishing.

Wahida Clark Presents Publishing
60 Evergreen Place Suite 904
East Orange, NJ 07018

www.wclarkpublishing.com

email: info@wclarkpublishing.com

Copyright 2020 © by Wahida Clark

ISBN 13-digit 978-1-947732-73-5 (Paperback)
ISBN 13-digit 978-19477321-8-6 (Hardback)
ISBN 13-digit 978-1-947732-74-2 (E-book)

Library of Congress Catalog Number: 2020943114

1. 1. Covid-19 2. Coronavirus Pandemic 3. Pandemic 4. Quarantine 5. Locckdown 6. Work From Home 7. Zoom 8. Social Media 9. Masks 10 I can't breathe

nuanceart@acreativenuance.com

Editorial Team: Natalie Sade and Phillip Smith

Printed in United States

Acknowledgments

To God Be All of the Praise and Glory!

Mike Sword, one of the most awesome entertainment attorneys I know. Thank you!! In the early part of this quarantine, you told me, "You should write a book COVID 19-related like only the Queen can. Hey, we are in lockdown anyway." I admit, I did laugh at first and shrugged it off. But we are blessed to have people on the team that when they talk, they at least take the time to go back and rewind. I'm sure glad I did.

A few months later . . . and here goes BOOK 1 of *My Quarantine Fantasy Series*. Thank you for being Mike Sword!

Dedication

To all of the Essential Personnel on the Front Lines. I never fully understood—until this pandemic—what "Front Line" and "Essential" truly meant. Thank you and much respect!

This work of fiction is also dedicated to bringing Love and Smiles during these (I call them *unbelievable*) times when Musical Therapy or Musical Mental Therapy is very much needed.

Follow @wahidaclark on Instagram and YouTube to View *The Queen of Street Lit Docuseries* and to attend Musical Aficionado Monday With Wahida Clark's *Street Lit House Party*, *Monologue Theater*, and the *SWAG R-Rated Cartoon Watch Party*.

Prologue

ANSINETTE

ANSINETTE NEVER THOUGHT she would meet a man that could make her feel so good. It seemed like she had an orgasm every time his skin brushed against hers. She had been with other men–men who proved to be boys when compared with this one. His lips were fire against her cool neck as he kissed her there, making her cringe from the sensation. His fondling hands pinched and pulled her tender flesh, kneading tight places that needed loosening. She gasped in delight and felt like screaming her joy. If her sons weren't in the other room playing video games, she would cry out declaring her satisfaction to all who cared to hear. But her sons were in the other room. There were some moments a mother was supposed to enjoy alone. She didn't want any rug-rats to spoil it. The boys had their time with her. Now it was her time for fun.

They lay beside each other, sprawled out on her bed. Her cotton pajamas bunched in all the wrong crevices, making her wish to rip them off. He wore a tank top and sweats that did nothing to prevent his excitement from jabbing her belly. Her natural hair was nappy and wrapped in the pink scarf she'd been wearing to bed since she was in college. She hadn't made up her face in days. Hadn't left the house in weeks. Not even for a walk. They'd woken up, ate breakfast, and did nothing for the rest of the morning. They hadn't showered yet, but it was okay. The lockdown exposed all secrets. There wasn't much she didn't know about him now. He was the man she wanted to be with. She was sure of it. Quarantining with someone was as close to marriage as two people could get.

Her eyes crept open. The noon sun perched high in a pale blue sky, spread golden stripes of light across the far wall of the open window. She stared out and did not spot a single cloud. The day's beauty reminded her of the beautiful way she felt while wrapped in his arms. He had a way of making her feel beautiful when she looked her worse. No man had ever made her so comfortable–so sure of herself.

He got up and stood at the foot of the bed. Ansinette stared as he pulled off his wife beater tank top. Breath caught in her throat; her eyes graced his tight chest and broad shoulders. His stomach rippled with bulging abs. She unbuttoned her pajama top but left the garment closed a bit to keep her decent. The COVID-19 weight she gained pooled around her belly and behind. She felt comfortable around him, but not that comfortable. He slipped his thumbs into the waistband of his sweatpants and slid them down. He wore no underwear. The sledgehammer she saw between his legs made her bottom lip quiver. Thinking of that long, hard black thing sliding in her made her forget her inhibitions.

"Marcus," she murmured.

He reached out and grabbed her pajama bottoms by the waist. Two strong yanks and they were floating high in the air toward the bedroom door. She wore pink granny panties beneath, and if he cared, he didn't show it. His huge hands spread her brown thighs wide as he climbed on the bed between them, where he laid all of his weight on top of her.

Ansinette's arms were wrapping around the back of Marcus' neck and pulling him down before she realized what she was doing. He responded with another kiss, this one planted softly on her lips. Their tongues mingled in the open space. Her eyes shut tight. Her pajama top slipped open, exposing her dark nipples to his hard chest. Their hearts beat in syncopation like horse hooves running wild toward the passion they both needed and wanted. Her hands roamed the expanse of his cobra-shaped back. Ansinette marveled at his muscles rippling beneath milk chocolate skin as he held her close. Her teeth sank into his shoulder to sample a taste.

"We can wait," he whispered. "If you want to. The boys are in the next room. Tonight is not too far away. They'll be asleep then."

Ansinette silenced him with a kiss. Her hand guided his beneath her panties to the flaming hot spot between her legs and let him feel how ready she was. His finger plunged inside as easily as a dolphin diving in a swimming pool. Ansinette kept her hand between them and gripped his manhood. It was so thick that her fingers barely stretched around it. She stroked him from the base to the tip. Her tongue snaked out and licked a circle around his earlobe. She moaned. He grunted. There would be no waiting today. Before he entered her, Ansinette smiled up at the ceiling. She couldn't help it. A million thoughts ran through her mind, and she couldn't focus on a single one. She tried in vain to pinpoint when she had fallen for him, but that moment was lost to her. So much had happened in so little time. It was as if she had read her story in a fairytale rather than lived it. He was perfect in each and every way. She couldn't believe they had been perfect strangers just two weeks ago.

The coronavirus pandemic had changed the course of their lives in many more ways than one. Lockdowns, riots, protests . . . thoughts of the last fourteen days whizzed by like a blur as Marcus kissed her again. She closed her eyes. For one precious second, all she thought of was the feeling of his lips against hers. When he pulled back, images of her working from a computer at home, homeschooling her kids, and losing her sanity while being stuck at home invaded her mind. Marcus' lips closed over a pert nipple. Her pains disappeared once again. They faded so far away that Ansinette closed her eyes tighter to keep them away. She was thankful that Marcus had been on lockdown with her. She could think of no other man she would have liked to spend that maddening and unpredictable time with.

Her hand pressed the tip of his manhood to her slick opening. She gasped as he slipped inside, inch by inch until he filled her up. Her legs draped behind his back as he sank his weight on top of her and settled in. He kissed her once again. His lips telling her how much he appreciated her love in ways that his mouth could never express.

Ansinette didn't want to think about all of the people who had died from the coronavirus or the people who lost their homes, their jobs, and their sanity. She didn't want to think about them, but she couldn't help it. They hated being locked down. Being quarantined had ruined their lives. It had not ruined Ansinette's.

Her arms pulled Marcus closer as he began pumping into her. As they made love, she couldn't help but think about the fateful day their lives changed forever.

One

MARCUS

MARCUS SAT ON THE BACK of the open U-Haul moving truck to catch his breath. Tony, his co-worker and friend, lugged a tall halogen lamp down the apartment steps. Both men wore homemade face masks to protect against the invisible and highly contagious virus that had sparked worldwide fear in every waking human being.

Tony stopped a few feet in front of Marcus and set down the lamp. "That's most of it. All you have left are a ton of boxes."

Marcus nodded. "Thanks, bro. I can handle everything else." Marcus slid off the truck to give Tony a quick elbow bump. "I appreciate you for coming by. I wouldn't have been able to move all of that stuff without your help."

"Remember when I got locked up down at Myrtle Beach? You drove all the way to South Carolina to bond me out. My wife never knew. I owed you this little bit of help." Marcus reached into his back pocket for his wallet. "Let me buy you gas and a burger for the ride home." Tony tossed his hands up, palms flat. "I'm good. You'll need that money. There's no telling what's about to happen out here. They're shutting the state down. They've already closed the barbershops. We might be going through this thing for a while." Marcus still reached into his wallet. "Tony. You've got two kids and a mortgage. We were both laid off today. Not just me."

"You don't have to remind me," Tony replied. "Tabitha makes enough money for both of us to get by. She's working from home, but at least she's working. We live in a small house, and both our cars are paid off. Our main expense is food. We'll be fine. She's at home cooking right now." He pointed to Marcus with a look of concern staining his face. "You-you're all alone. Hold on to that bread. You need it more than me." Tony turned and headed toward his car, a late model nineties sedan.

Marcus watched him open the door. He took a glance inside the open wallet idling in his hands. Two ten-dollar bills rubbed faces. It wasn't all the money he had, but he had to admit that he needed every dime.

Just before Tony slid inside his car, Marcus called out, "Thanks Tony! I'll see you back at work soon!"

Tony paused and looked back with a frown crinkling his face. "I hope it's sooner than later." He sat down, then stood again to face Marcus. "You know you can sleep on my couch, right? I've got a man cave over the garage. PlayStation One through Four. I even have the old Nintendo with Zelda and Contra. You can stay with us for as long as you need to."

Marcus lowered his eyes and focused on the parking lot pavement as he shook his head.

Tony nodded in acceptance. "I didn't think you would take me up. Just know that you've got a place to go if you need it."

Marcus offered no reply. He stood still as Tony climbed back in his car and drove off, yet Marcus wondered what great deed he had done to deserve such a friend. Although he appreciated the offer, he couldn't see himself imposing on a married man and his family. A man should be able to take care of himself. He shouldn't have to depend on his friends for help, especially when he put himself in the troubled position.

He lowered his face mask to breathe in fresh air and looked up at his apartment door hanging open. Well, his old apartment, it wasn't his anymore. Despite the messed-up way he felt inside, he swore to make his new situation work, no matter what hardship he had to face.

His phone rang. Marcus looked at the Caller ID and cursed. It was his mother. Betty. He answered reluctantly. "Hey, Mama . . . "

"Hey yourself. Why haven't you called me? I was watching CNN and I heard the governor of North Carolina say that he's shutting down the state. He's closing everything. Restaurants. Bars. Businesses. When were you going to call to tell me?"

"I–I didn't want to worry you."

She laughed. "I'm in California. You're across the country in the Jim Crow south where they're killing black boys every damn day. They just shot one for jogging down the street in Georgia, Marcus. Said they *thought* he was committing a crime. I'm going to worry if the sun is bright and the sky is clear. Life has taught me that there's always a storm brewing somewhere, and I pray that it doesn't rain on your head."

Marcus couldn't argue with that. "'I should have called, but I just found out myself. They were talking about a curfew at first. We all thought a state shutdown was a rumor until today."

"What about your job," she asked.

That was the one question he'd been dreading. A part of him wished he could forget about it. He didn't want to tell his mother the truth about what happened. She would overreact and offer to do something rash. Then again, he didn't want to lie to her. His lying days were over.

"They shut down already," he said. Marcus listened. Her end remained dangerously silent. "It's a meat packing plant. People work less than a foot apart. It's impossible to practice social distancing. Somebody on first shift got sick, and they tested everybody. Eighty percent of the plant tested positive. They laid me off with a text this morning."

Betty groaned. "Marcus, I loved that job for you."

"I know."

Smithfield Packing hired Marcus as a floor laborer sweeping up meat scraps for seven-seventy-five an hour. It was the best job he could find after getting out of prison. Black ex-felons found it difficult to climb corporate ladders. To show his appreciation, he arrived on time every day, worked late when they needed him, and he never complained. A month later, they promoted him to cutter on the line. Two months after that, he made Assistant Shift

Manager. The promotion to Shift Manager came two weeks ago. His mother's pride invigorated him, but no one loved his progress more than he did.

"Are you sick?" she asked next.

"No. Surprisingly. My test came back negative."

"I hope you got down on your knees and thanked the Lord. How are you looking on money?"

Marcus let out a sigh. "I've got something saved up."

"How much?"

"Mama . . ."

"Marcus, I changed your shitty-ass draws for two years. You ain't hiding nothing from me."

He gritted his teeth. "I've got a little over four-thousand in the bank."

Silence. And then, "That's good. I'm proud of you. You might need every penny. Is your rent paid up? Your light bill?"

Marcus glanced up at his apartment. His old apartment. Moving out seemed like a good idea when he'd made the decision two days ago. But under his mother's scrutiny things looked a little worse. "My lease ran out yesterday. I didn't renew it. I was moving out when you called."

"Where are you moving to? Your state is going on lock-down. Are you telling me that there is an apartment complex accepting new tenants during a worldwide pandemic?"

He stumbled over his words when he tried to answer. He was twenty-nine-years-old, but Betty always made him feel like the pre-teen who'd been caught stealing cigarettes from the gas station up the street. He never knew what to say, and what spewed out of his mouth fell short of adequacy.

A silver Dodge Charger rumbled around the corner and

parked four empty spaces away.

Two young boys spilled out of the backseat. Anthony was the oldest. His younger brother, David, was nine. Their mother, Ansinette, climbed out of the driver's seat. One glimpse of her made Marcus forget whatever he was saying into the phone.

Ansinette wore her dark chocolate skin like an extravagant fur coat that every other woman in the world should envy. Her face held none of the features mainstream media defined as beautiful. Her round nose spread wide, perfectly situated between her thick, soft lips and her slanted eyes. They squinted slyly as she smiled at him from across the parking lot. Today she bound her natural tresses in a burgundy scarf tied like a bandana across her forehead. Weak minded men under the programming of white standards of beauty, wouldn't recognize her flawlessness, but she was breathtakingly beautiful to him. Oiled and sandaled feet carried her to the trunk of her car. She wore a sleeveless beige dress with a plunging neckline. Nothing elegant. Just something to wear to the store.

Marcus couldn't take his eyes away from the sway of her hips beneath the thin dress, or the way her breasts stretched the fabric.

"Marcus!" His mother screamed in his ear.

"Yeah, yeah. What was your question again?"

"Where are you going to sleep? It sounds like you're homeless."

Marcus listened, but his focus remained locked on Ansinette opening her trunk. "I'll be fine, Mama. I've got friends willing to help me out."

"Mm-hm. Be careful who you trust, remember you did five years in a North Carolina prison behind people you thought you could trust. Calling me every month for money. Shit. Putting money on your books was like paying a damn bill."

"Mama."

"Marcus. Let me send you an airplane ticket. You can save your money by staying with me for a while. At least until this corona thing is over."

Marcus stared as Ansinette's boys bolted past him. "Hey, Mr. Jenkins!" They yelled in unison. He smiled while watching them bound up the stairs toward their apartment, directly across from his. He noted that they had not offered to help their mother with the groceries. Ansinette looked his way and cocked her head to the side with a frown. He wondered why she gazed at him with such a sour expression, until he thought of the moving truck behind him.

His mother said, "I want to help you, Marcus. You've come so far since you were released from prison. I don't want you to go back. If you end up in a bad situation . . ."

"I'm not going back to prison, Mama. I promise you that. Don't worry about me. I'll get through this just fine."

Ansinette pulled two full paper sacks from her trunk and started walking toward Marcus. "Mama, look . . . I have to go. I'll call you later, okay." Betty was still yelling in his ear as he hung up and smiled at Ansinette. "Hey," he said as she approached. "How are you today?"

Ansinette glanced at the moving truck before looking back at Marcus. "I was fine until I saw this loaded moving van. Are you tired of me already? I didn't know I stank that bad."

Marcus chuckled. Her sense of humor attracted him almost as much as her beauty. He noticed her staring at his face mask. No mask shielded her face. She took two huge steps back.

Marcus shrugged. "Who stinks now?" He pulled the mask back up over his lips and nose. "Social distancing," she replied. "I forgot. So many new rules. Can't leave your house without a mask and gloves. Can't touch anything at the store. Wash your hands and incinerate your clothes when you get home. It's all so exhausting."

He nodded in agreement. "They say it's for our own good."

Ansinette studied his eyes for a moment. "Why are you moving? I thought you liked it here."

"I do . . . " he began.

After his release from prison, North Carolina forced him to live in the state to finish his twelve-month post-release. Briarcliff Apartments in Cary was the only complex that would lease him a place fresh out of prison. It hurt his eyes to look at the ancient brick buildings, but the neighborhood was quiet, and criminals stayed away. He'd spent two peaceful years in his cozy one-bedroom apartment.

"My lease ended yesterday," he admitted. "The front office offered me a chance to renew it, but my rent would have gone up two hundred dollars a month. I don't want to pay that for the same apartment. That . . . and I got laid off from my job."

"Oh no."

"I saw it coming. I figured they would shut down."

Ansinette's face sagged. "I hate to hear that they're raising the rent, though. If they did it to you, what about the rest of us?"

Marcus held up a hand to stop her from panicking. "Only when your lease is up, as far as I know."

Ansinette's eyes graced the open truck with Marcus' belongings packed neatly inside. "You find someplace cheaper?"

"Nah, not yet. I could have renewed my lease, but I want to live somewhere better if I'm going to pay more. Besides, I haven't had time to look for another apartment. Then with this lockdown. No apartment offices are open."

Ansinette nodded with understanding. "You're stuck in the middle. Damn. So what are you going to do?"

Marcus peered inside the truck. "Put all my stuff in storage and sleep in my car." Ansinette laughed a little. When Marcus didn't laugh too, she took a serious look at him.

"You're really going to sleep in your car?"

"A couple of weeks won't kill me. Once everything opens again, I'll be okay."

Ansinette's blank stare told him that she wasn't so convinced. Marcus hated to see her wearing pity in her eyes. She and her boys had been living across the hall from him for six or seven months. He liked her the first time they'd met in the parking lot—just like this—but she seemed like such a good girl that he decided not to rush her into anything back then. She didn't act entitled to his money or cop an attitude when he said something she didn't agree with, like a lot of women he'd dated. Their conversations were casual. They shared greetings like, "Hey, how ya doin'?" while they climbed in their cars for work in the mornings. Sometimes they took walks around the neighborhood. They were a little more than friends, but a lot less than lovers. He felt that she liked him too, but early in their friendship she explained that she had just ended a long-term relationship with the father of her children and was enjoying being single. Marcus decided not to press her after that. He figured that she would let him know if she wanted to take their relationship further.

Ansinette's lips pursed. "I think you should renew your lease. Even if ifs only for a few months."

Marcus shook his head. "My job closed down. I don't know when they'll open back up. If I renew my lease and I can't work, I'll eat up my savings."

"Damn, Marcus. If you didn't plan on spending it, why did you save the money?"

"To buy a house."

She laughed again. "Who are you going to live with in a big old house?"

"Myself. I want to own something. I'm tired of spending money to live in a dump someone can kick me out of or raise my rent whenever they feel like it. I want something with my name on it." He smiled behind the mask. "If I can find a woman to love me then she can live there too."

Ansinette smirked. "I bet. She'll be paying half of the house note too, huh?"

"Nah. She won't have to pay. But she'll do the dishes and wash my draws. Everybody has to earn their keep."

Ansinette smacked her lips. "You better hope she's better than me. Your funky little draws will stand up and walk across the room singing the national anthem before I put my hands on them, if you come in my house talking like that. Talking about washing dishes. You better learn how to wash some paper plates."

Marcus' long and hearty laugh made him rock from side to side and forget about the troubles weighing him down. He didn't care about the neighborhood or the apartment. He wasn't attached to any of those things. He could have moved out long ago and found another complex. He'd been out of prison long enough to establish his credit. He stayed because Ansinette lived across the hall from him, and he couldn't bear to leave. If he missed anything, he would miss her.

Ansinette's smile faded. "You're a man with dreams. I can respect that. Even if your plans are a little crazy."

"Small dreams. Manageable dreams."

"What tree doesn't begin as a seed? What river didn't begin as a trickling stream?"

"You're a poet?"

She smiled at that. "You're moving. You'll never know."

Marcus strode a little closer to Ansinette, but not too close. "Just because I'm leaving doesn't mean I can't see you." Marcus raised an eyebrow. "I know where you live."

Ansinette recoiled. "You sound like one of those creepy Lifetime movies: Stalked at Fifteen. I should have done a background check on you."

"Seriously, Ansinette. I want to come back and see you. You've been a good neighbor."

"Is that it? Just a neighbor?"

"You've been a good friend too."

She heaved her grocery bags a little higher. "You can come around, but Marcus, I can't believe you're serious about living in your car. Isn't that a little extreme? I know you want to save money, but there has to be a better way than that. It's just like a man to do something insane. Got a whole grocery store on the corner, yet you want to go hunting and shit."

Marcus hated to admit that she was right. Living in his car did seem a little over the top. "I've got some friends," he told her. "Somebody will take me in. I don't need much."

Ansinette started to reply, but her boys appeared at the top of the stairs. Anthony shouted, "Mom, hurry up. We're hungry."

David rubbed his belly. "My ribs is touching my back!"

Ansinette frowned up at them. "Your ribs *are* touching your back!" She responded, then turned to Marcus. "Well, I've got to go before they start gnawing on the couch."

Marcus saw her heft the bags in her arms once more. "Let me take those." He reached out and plucked them from her grip. He started toward the stairs. "I'll follow you in the house and bring up the rest. Go ahead and feed your boys." Marcus waited for her to head toward the stairs too, but she stood stock still while staring at him. Her silence unnerved him. "Ansinette? What?"

Two

ANSINETTE

THE MORNING SUN BEAMED into the bedroom as Ansinette stared at the phone in her hand. Her sister Robin glared back with her lips tight, awaiting an answer.

"Ansinette."

"Robin, it's only for a little while. This whole thing will be over soon. It's not that big of a deal."

Robin rolled her eyes. "You invited a stranger to live in your home. A man you are not dating. That's a big deal."

Ansinette walked to her closet and shoved clothes around on their hangers, searching for something to wear. Without Marcus there, she could lounge in her pajamas all day. Not now. She needed to be conscious of her every decision. Her appearance never mattered so much before.

She pushed a sweater aside and remembered that it was April and she needed to bag up her winter clothes. Just one

THE VIRUS BROUGHT ME MY FIRST LOVE

more task to add to her COVID-19 checklist. "He's not a stranger, Robin. I've known him for almost a year. He lived across the hall. We're friends."

Robin thought about it. "Are you talking about the muscular brother that drives the big truck? The black Dodge Ram?"

Ansinette nodded. "Marcus. The one you said you'd let creep up in all your little crevices."

Robin paused. "I didn't say that."

"You did. You also invited him to dinner and told him he wouldn't have to pay for the condoms later."

"I don't remember that. Besides, I had been drinking Hennessey. You know how I get when I'm sipping yack. There isn't a safe penis within a ten-mile radius." Robin declared. "I think that was the weekend I'd just come back from my business trip in Colorado. Those edibles were kicking my ass. But that doesn't mean he's safe. People live next door to serial rapists for decades without knowing how they bury bodies in their cabbage garden."

"He doesn't have a cabbage garden." Ansinette stopped her wardrobe search to stare at the phone. "He's not a rapist. He's a nice guy."

"So was Jeffery Dahmer. Ted Bundy was a freaking clown at children's parties."

Ansinette jerked out a pair of jeans and a yellow blouse. "Whatever."

"Where is he sleeping anyway? You don't have room for a grown man in that matchbox you call an apartment."

Ansinette quickly laid her clothes out on the bed. She sat down on the edge and looked at her sister on the phone's screen. "Anthony and David share a room. I haven't been able to buy David his own bed. Anthony has the bunk beds, so David sleeps in there. Marcus rolled out a sleeping bag on the floor last night. All his furniture is in storage. He brought a couple boxes of clothes and stuff. He says it'll be fine."

"I'll bet. He's two paces away from the inside of your panties. He's probably in that thing fantasizing about you right now. You might want to check it for stains."

"Robin!"

Robin giggled. "Sis, you've got to be careful. Coronavirus isn't the only thing a girl has to worry about. You haven't had any D in a while and you're thinking with your v-jay-jay, but baby, be careful. Letting some man live with you is a lot different than having a one-night stand. It doesn't matter how much you like him."

"Who says I like him?"

"You let him move into your apartment."

Ansinette blew out a long sigh. "Is it that obvious? I can't help it, Robin. He's sooo fine. He's got that athletic body and peanut colored skin. Damn. I couldn't let him sleep in his car. That wouldn't have been right. And just because he's staying here doesn't mean we'll get something going. Sex is the last thing on my mind."

"What else are you going to do? Y'all are going to be stuck in the house for only God knows how long."

Ansinette met her sister's eyes. "Jealous?"

"The only man I need takes C batteries in his backside. Harold is the best man I've ever loved. I don't have to get out of bed if I don't want to. I don't have to feed him. I don't have to wash his clothes. I don't even have to wash my ass. All I have to do is roll over and click him on. Harold touches me just how I like it and anytime I need it."

Ansinette howled a long laugh. "Girl, you are silly."

Robin patted her natural hair. "Look at my hair. I didn't even pick it out this morning. Do you think Harold cares?"

"It looks like a mushroom cloud wrapped in a rubber band."

Robin nodded. "Now ask me if I give a damn. I have a meeting online in an hour. I'll comb my hair later. Until then, it's just me and my vibrator."

Ansinette's smile faded. "He's not my man, Robin. We're just friends."

"Is that right? What's Devon going to say when he finds out about Marcus?"

Devon had not crossed Ansinette's mind. Her children's father lived in another town, forty minutes away. He popped up when he was in the neighborhood or if he wanted some sex.

He never stopped by just to see his sons. He sent a child support check once a month, but he offered no other help.

Ansinette rolled her eyes. "I don't care what he thinks. I'm sure he's got some little strumpet to occupy his time."

"Oh, I didn't tell you that I saw him at Crabtree Valley the other day, did I?

"You sent me a text, but ..."

"Girl. He was walking with this little dumpy white girl. She was as wide as she was tall. She had long red hair and enough blue eyeliner to get a part in *Braveheart*."

It never bothered Ansinette to know that Devon saw other women. They had lived together for over ten years, and he cheated on her the entire time. She didn't think he knew what the word monogamous meant. They met in college. He was finishing up his law degree when she was enrolling as a freshman. She and Robin had grown up without a father in the house. Devon, the older man, filled that role easily. He worked, owned a car, and paid his bills on time. Ansinette couldn't have asked for more in a man. Most of the young men she dated were selling drugs or doing them, and they always expected a portion of her paycheck. Devon proved to be the closest thing to stability she had ever known. They moved in together when she got pregnant with Anthony. She caught him fucking her best friend on their couch a week after they signed the lease to their first apartment. She forgave him and stayed, and that became a recurrence throughout the decade plus that they were together.

Ansinette glanced at the time in the corner of her phone's screen. She had a meeting soon too. "Devon will be Devon. I'm glad I realized it when I did. I wish I had realized it sooner."

"Yeah, well, he and Becky seemed really happy together."

"I'm glad he's with her," Ansinette confessed. "Maybe it'll stop him from sniffing around my door."

"He's still trying to get with you?"

Ansinette smacked her lips. "Every time his mouth opens."

Robin took a long look at her sister. "You gave him some, didn't you?"

"So what if I did?"

"Ansinette."

"What? It's my body, I can do what I want. We were arguing about the child support check again. He kept holding it over my head. I needed to pay for Anthony's Kung Fu lessons, and David needed some new shoes. He came over here one night with some Seagram's Seven and orange juice. He started talking really nice and rubbing on my leg. Shit. I wanted it too. He might not be much of a man, but he knows how to get me started. If he hadn't been cheating, we'd still be together."

Robin massaged her temples. "Is that what you tell yourself to justify acting like a damned fool? You'll never get rid of him if you keep sleeping with him. You still love him, don't you?"

"I don't know. I miss him."

Robin frowned as if she had sucked a sour lemon. "He's always holding that child support over your head. How do you know he's not doing that just so he can wedge his way into your panties? He thinks he's so slick. If you want him out of your life, you're going to have to get rid of him for good. Stop being nice. Stop fucking him. You're acting just like Mommy. Letting a man treat you how he wants to. Remember how Sammy used to come in the house all hours of the night? She'd wait up for him mad and pacing the floor, swearing that this time was the last time. But when he walked in the door smelling like beer and vagina, she'd let him inside with the same stupid look that's plastered across your face right now. Not me. I'd rather be all by my damn self than put up with that shit."

"Robin . . ."

"Stop being so weak. You've got a great job. You can do better. You should do better. If you keep giving him what he wants, he'll keep treating you like a dog. He just wants to sleep with you. That's why he plays games with your money."

Ansinette had to admit that Robin was right. She allowed Devon to run all over her. Their mother set a bad example by permitting Sammy, their stepfather, to abuse her in the same way. Sammy didn't leave until Ansinette and Robin were in their teens. By then, the damage was done.

Honestly, Ansinette feared trying to find someone else. When she looked in the mirror, she didn't see the features she equated with beauty. She saw a plain black woman that men overlooked when some light-skinned heifer passed. Why would a man want her? Her hair was nappy. Her skin was purple-black. Her booty was too wide. Her breasts too large and pendulous. Her tummy too round. Boys ignored her in high school. They chased cheerleaders and fast white girls. Devon wanted her. At least that was something. Then again, she couldn't wait for him to decide he needed to treat her better.

"I'll think about it," she told Robin.

"The next time he threatens to hold your child support check, have him locked up. See if Becky with the red hair will bail his ass out of there. He might realize that he likes men instead."

"I can't have him locked up, Robin."

"I don't see why not. Don't be scared to show him what the inside of the Wake County jail looks like. Be short with your money and let him see what you can do. Orange is the new broke, Ansinette. I'm not playing. Them boys ain't free to raise! Don't play with his ass. Those boys need a stable environment."

"They need their father too."

Robin scoffed at that. "You act like he's coming over there to play catch with them. He ain't nowhere to be seen. All he does is write a check, and he won't even do that on time. No. You need to hold him accountable for his actions." Robin stopped and squinted in the distance as she thought about something. "You moving that man into your house may let him know that he doesn't have as tight a hold on you as he thinks he does. A little jealousy never hurt anybody." Ansinette felt her heart beat faster. "Marcus is only staying until this lockdown is over."

"So what? Devon doesn't know that. Do you think that'll cross his mind if he sees a young, strapping man prancing around your house with his shirt off? Looking like a caramel Morris Chestnut. He won't believe the truth if you explain it to him. Use that to your advantage."

"How, Robin? I don't know how to play games with people."

"I don't think you'll have to play games. If he finds out, he'll draw his own conclusions."

Ansinette held her head low. "Let's hope the coronavirus leaves us before that can happen." She checked the time again. "Look, I have to get breakfast going before my meeting, Robin. I'll call you later."

"If I don't pick up, I'll be with my boyfriend." Robin held up a large black vibrator in the shape of an oversized penis, complete with a head and veins. She clicked it on. Ansinette giggled as it buzzed. Robin held the toy close to her ear. "Harold says, hello."

Ansinette ended the call and started dressing, nervous to face Marcus.

Three

MARCUS

IT WAS A DREAM. He knew it. She stood before him wearing only a white thong and push-up bra. Her dark skin singed his fingertips as if he had drenched his finger in a cup of boiling, hot coffee. She smiled at his touch. He pulled her close. His hands sank down to the soft mounds of her round behind. Her tongue tasted sugary like candy. His manhood yearned to slide inside of her as they inched even closer.

Something banged against the door, jarring him awake. His legs scrambled to carry him to a standing position, but he soon realized that he lay encased in a sleeping bag, not beneath loose blankets in his own bed. His eyes shot open to the foreign bedroom. He saw a collection of G.I. Joe's standing atop a toy chest beside him. Seconds later, a woman's voice echoed in the hallway beyond the closed door. "Boy!

I told you not to throw that football in my house! I told you that we have company!" Marcus heard a series of slaps, then crying.

The door opened. Ansinette poked her head inside the room. She wore a radiant smile instead of the angry scowl he expected. "Good morning," she said. "I'm sorry if David woke you."

Marcus squeezed his legs together to hide his erection, then he realized that she couldn't see it through the sleeping bag. "It's okay. I needed to get up anyway. I have to check on some things."

"Are you hungry? I was going to make the boys something. You're welcome to join us. I mean, it's not like you can drive to McDonald's."

"They're open."

Her smile faded. "You're not going out there."

Marcus grinned. "Let me wash up. I'll eat with you guys."

Ansinette bit her lip before pulling back and closing the door.

Marcus laid his head back on the pillow. Thoughts of her kept a smile spread across his face. Her lingering scent wafted to his nose, smelling like an endless field of wildflowers blowing in a spring breeze. His eyes squeezed shut again. He tried in vain to summon his fading dream of her, but its remnants faded into a murky haze. He remembered her face, but no more, yet his erection raged on. Slowly his hand crept beneath the sleeping bag to grip his manhood.

His hand moved up and down as he massaged himself to thoughts of Ansinette. Her image came back to him. She stood before him. His hand became her hand. Her lips brushed against his neck.

His fist pumped faster beneath the sleeping bag. He imagined laying her on a bed and slipping between her legs. Pleasure rose within him. A momentous orgasm threatened to take him over the edge when a second thud banged against the door.

His eyes shot open. The G.I. Joe's on the toy chest gaped at him. One pointed a rifle his way. "What are you doing?" He asked himself, removing his hand from beneath the sleeping bag.

His phone rang as soon as he unzipped and stood up. He answered dryly. "What's up, Mama?"

"Did you find a place to live yet?"

Marcus ran a hand over his bald head. "You're not going to let this go, are you?"

"Not until I know you're okay."

"At least you're consistent."

"Well?"

"I moved in with my neighbor. Ansinette. She has an extra bedroom and let me sleep here until I can find a place. It shouldn't take too long. Couple of weeks. Just until this coronavirus lockdown is over."

"Ansinette." Betty spat the name like a bite of rancid meat. "You're too old to be shacking up with some strange woman, Marcus."

"We're not shacking up, Mama."

"Hmph, are you paying rent?"

Marcus cracked his neck. "She hasn't mentioned it. No."

"Sounds like shacking up to me."

"She did me a favor, Mama. We're friends. We've lived across the hall from each other for almost a year now. You met her at Christmas."

Betty went silent on her end. "You mean that black thing with the two crumb snatchers that tried to steal my purse in the parking lot?"

Marcus rubbed his tired eyes. Every conversation with his mother was the equivalent to a twelfth round with Mike Tyson. "They weren't stealing your purse. Your rental car was the same model and color as Ansinette's car. They thought your car was hers."

"What else would you expect a pack of thieves to say?"

"Mama, look. I need to hop in the shower."

"Alright; but let me remind you that men shed like dogs in the shower. Make sure you clean that woman's tub when you finish. No woman wants to love a nasty man."

Marcus paused to make sure he heard her correctly. "She doesn't want me, Mama."

Betty clucked her tongue. "You can lie to yourself about what you're doing there, but you can't lie to your mother."

The phone went dead in his ear.

Ten minutes later, he headed to the shower. Ansinette rushed from the kitchen at the same time and bumped into him. He stood shirtless in a pair of gym shorts. He noticed her eyes linger over his muscular torso a moment too long.

She frowned, "Is that how you're coming to breakfast?"

Marcus smiled at her obvious discomfort. "No. This is how I'm going to the shower."

"Oh," she muttered, then scrunched her eyebrows. "Maybe you should put on a shirt. I wouldn't want my boys to get the wrong idea."

"What idea is that?"

She looked up into his eyes and licked her lips. "You know, that me and you, you know what. Just put on a shirt please."

Marcus didn't move a muscle. "For the boys."

Ansinette started toward her bedroom. "For the boys." She turned back briefly and looked him up and down once more before disappearing into the room.

Marcus laughed to himself and went back to his room to put on a T-shirt.

After his shower, Marcus entered the dining room and adjoining kitchen in a pair of jeans and a tank top. Ansinette stood at the stove stirring what smelled like a pot of grits. Anthony and David sat at the kitchen table amidst a mountain of textbooks and writing paper. Anthony swiped his finger across the screen of a tablet, while his brother David looked at him jealously. No one noticed Marcus standing there.

David leaned over Anthony's shoulder, peering at the tablet. "Let me see it, Anthony."

"Go get yours. I'm busy."

David snatched the tablet from Anthony. "You broke mine, remember?"

Anthony raised his hand to slap David.

David recoiled and clutched the tablet to his chest. "Mama!"

Ansinette glanced up from her grits long enough to mutter. "Anthony, if you hit that boy, I will knock you through that wall. I don't have time to play with you today." As an afterthought she said, "You need to be doing your schoolwork anyway. Pass/Fail does not mean that you don't have to do the work."

David stuck out his tongue at Anthony. "That's right. Do your homework."

Marcus leaned against the doorframe and crossed his

arms. A slight smile spread across his lips. Ansinette moved around the kitchen cracking eggs, whipping them, and stirring grits, amazingly at the same time. Her phone rang. She glanced at the Caller ID and picked it up on the second ring. "Guuurl!" she said. "This COVID-19 is about to drive me stir crazy. Did you see what they said on the news about it mutating?"

Anthony pulled an open textbook in front of him and pouted at the words without reading. Marcus saw a bit of himself in the boy. He'd hated school too when he was young. He loved being outside with a football in his hands.

Marcus looked back to Ansinette. She told whoever was on the phone that she had a meeting soon. She was waiting for her boss to chime in online for it. Marcus admired her grace. His eyes crawled from her bare feet, up her round calves, past her plump thighs, and to an ass straining against skinny jeans. The baggy canary blouse she wore hid her curves up top, but the sight of her jiggling beneath made his mouth water. The kind of beauty she possessed didn't derive from a hairdo or name brand clothing. It wasn't a carbon copy of some model in a magazine. Ansinette's beauty was born of her being. She exuded perfection no matter what clothes she wore or how she wore them. Her beauty was defined by its own standards.

A computer chimed down the hall behind him.

Marcus cleared his throat. All three sets of eyes turned to him. Everything went silent. Even the boiling pot of grits. "Your computer is ringing."

Ansinette came to life in a torrent of jerky movements as she struggled to turn off the grits, hang up the phone, and stop everything else she was doing at once.

Marcus walked over to her. "Do you need a hand?"

She waved him off. "No, I've got it." She moved the grits from the flaming stove eye to a cool one and seemed undecided about what task she should do next.

Marcus took the wooden spoon from her hand and moved to the stove. "Answer your computer. They won't wait all day."

Ansinette stared at him blankly, but she didn't protest. "Thank you." She hurried toward the back hall. "Welcome to my crazy life!" She called out over her shoulder.

Marcus buttered a skillet to scramble eggs. He noticed Anthony and David staring at him.

When he looked back at them, they turned away. He peered over Anthony's shoulder. "What are you studying, champ?"

Anthony rolled his eyes. "Nothing."

David spun in his seat. "History. Mama says he's going to fail because he doesn't study."

Anthony glared at his little brother. Marcus kept his focus on Anthony.

"Are you reading about a time period or a person?"

He noticed the Asian figure wearing battle armor on the open page of Anthony's textbook.

Anthony crossed his arms over his chest. "Some old Chinese dude named Genghis Khan. I don't know why we have to read about him. He's been dead for a thousand years. He didn't even have the internet."

Marcus stirred the grits to make sure they didn't stick as they cooled. "What? Genghis Khan was one of the greatest conquerors to ever live. And he wasn't Chinese. He was a Mongol. They were a nomadic people who traveled in the freezing mountains of Mongolia. They lived in little huts called Gers. His father was killed, and Genghis' family was abandoned by their tribe, who left them in the wilderness to die. Genghis was about your age then."

Anthony turned in his chair to listen. "They were homeless?"

"Pretty much. He rose from there to become emperor of a land holding almost twice the size of China."

Anthony's eyes widened. "China's the biggest country on Earth."

Marcus dropped two slices of bread in the toaster. "Tell me about it."

Anthony opened his mouth to speak, but they all paused when Ansinette screamed, "Damn!" from her bedroom. Marcus dropped everything and ran to her.

"What's wrong?" he asked as he entered her bedroom. The boys remained at the door. She sat behind her computer rubbing her forehead. "I can't get this stupid Zoom thing to work. I logged into the meeting. I turned the camera and the sound on, but they can't hear me, and I can't hear them. What am I going to do? I have a presentation and—what am I going to do?"

"Don't panic." Marcus stepped behind her and looked at the computer screen. A dozen white faces in little boxes stared back at him from the comfort of their homes. None of them were talking. He didn't know what Ansinette did for work, but it must have been important. They were all waiting for her. He grabbed her mouse. "Sometimes Zoom wants to act up. If you can't hear anything, go here." Marcus clicked a downward pointing arrow in the left-hand corner. A menu box popped up. "When you get here click test *speaker and microphone*." He clicked it. A series of bells chimed. He clicked *finished*, then leaned his face close to the screen. "Can you guys hear me?"

Five people smiled brightly and replied, "Yes. Now we can hear you."

Marcus backed away and left Ansinette smiling as he walked out and closed the door behind him. Anthony and David followed him back to the kitchen.

Marcus poured the beaten eggs into the skillet. He stirred the grits. He pressed the bread in the toaster.

Anthony asked, "What were you saying about Genghis Khan?"

Marcus smiled. "So now you're interested in history?"

David added. "Me too. I like this Genghis Khan."

"I'm glad. But even though Genghis was a great man, he was no hero. In fact, there's a legend that says he killed his brother."

David and Anthony looked at each other.

"That's right," Marcus continued. "Genghis and another brother shot him up with arrows."

David gulped. "Why did they do that?"

Marcus looked at the tablet in David's hands. "Because he took something from him."

David slid the tablet on the kitchen table in front of Anthony.

Marcus shoveled eggs and grits onto three plates. "When Genghis and his family lived in the wild, he was forced to hunt for food. Anything he killed had to be shared between five of them, even if it was a small rabbit. But each time he got food, his brother beat him up, took it, and ate it by himself while everyone else starved. It wasn't right, but Genghis knew that sharing was the only way his family was going to survive. There was no room for anyone to be greedy."

"That's messed up," Anthony blurted.

"Don't take a lesson from what he did to his brother, but why he did it. Family has to stick together." The toast popped up golden and delicious looking. "You guys want jelly?"

Anthony answered for them both. "Yes, Mr. Jenkins."

"Call me. Marcus."

Anthony smiled at that. "How do you know so much?"

Marcus slid their full plates in front of them. "I studied in school. Even if I didn't like what I was forced to learn, I found something that I liked about it. No matter what it was."

David took a bite of his toast. "Will you tell us more about Genghis Khan?" Marcus shook his head. "Nope, the next time we talk, you'll tell me about him." Anthony slid his textbook close and read as he ate his breakfast.

Four

ANSINETTE

ANSINETTE AWOKE TO HER RINGING PHONE. The sun had just crested over the horizon and painted the morning sky in shades of orange and purple. She preferred to wake with the rising sun. Her mother used to say that if a person started their day well it would end well. The wisdom proved true on most days, if not all.

She looked at her phone with sleepy eyes while still lying down. It was a FaceTime from Robin. When she answered, she noticed dark bags beneath Robin's eyes. Her natural hair was in disarray, and it looked as if she hadn't slept.

"Robin, what's wrong?"

Robin dabbed her eyes with a wadded tissue. "This damn coronavirus! It's ruining my life!"

Ansinette sat up in bed. "What happened?"

"I drove to the store late last night to get some things, you know. It was about two a.m. I hoped to beat the rush. Well . . . " She paused to sniffle. "I searched and searched, but they were all out. I couldn't believe it. I walked around every department in a panic." She trembled as a fresh wave of tears carried her over the edge. "How could they have run out? They're not supposed to run out."

"Robin, slow down, baby. Do you need toilet paper? I've got an extra bottle of bleach. I have sanitizer and wipes. What do you need? Let me know. I'll drop by your place and leave it on the doorstep."

"No," Robin whined. "I have all that."

Ansinette shrugged. "What are you crying about?"

"Batteries, Ansinette. They ran out of C batteries. I guess everybody needed them for flashlights or whatever. These crazy white folks are expecting a black uprising when we're all afraid of the flu. What the hell?"

"Batteries? What do you need batteries for?"

Robin gasped. She whipped out her vibrator. "Harold." Her lower lip quivered when she looked at it. "He-he died on me last night."

"Robin, are you serious?"

"Hell yes I'm serious! This could be catastrophic. Do you know how long we're going on lockdown? The governor was on the news last night talking about two whole months. I can't stay in this house all alone without Harold. I'll go crazy."

If Ansinette wasn't so upset, she would have laughed. "I know you didn't wake me up out of bed at seven in the morning about a damn vibrator. Girl, bye."

"Ansinette."

"I'm hanging up this phone."

"Don't you hang up on me. I'm your big sister. I helped Mama raise you."

"Robin, you're burning up all my data with this nonsense."

"What do you want me to do? I don't have a live-in penis like you. I've got to do what I can to stay sane up in here. I'm thirty-nine, Ansinette. Forty is a step in front of me. I need pleasure. Listen to him . . . " Robin clicked the vibrator on. It buzzed for a second then fizzled to silence. "This can't be happening to me." She whined.

Ansinette stared at her sister in disbelief. "You have an electric toothbrush, right? The kind with the round back?"

"Yeah, but how does that solve ..." Robin thought about it. "Hey. That just might do the trick. I'll call you back." Robin ended the call.

Ansinette stared at the phone in her hand and shook her head . . . "A live-in penis like me, huh?" She moved to toss the phone on the bed when another call came through. She answered and put the phone to her ear without looking at the Caller ID. "Robin, if you called to tell me that the electric toothbrush gave you a better orgasm than Harold, I'm hanging up!" A man's chuckle on the other end made her pause. "Devon?"

"If I had known it was going to be that kind of conversation, I would have worn my swimming trunks."

"I don't know what for. You don't turn anybody on. And you aren't doing any swimming in my panties."

"Aw, come on, Ansinette. You miss me. Admit it."

"Devon, how could I not miss arguing every minute of every day? How could I not miss finding strange women's underwear in your car? How could I not miss waiting up for you to come home until six in the morning? Ask me if I miss you again. I double dare you. I've got another list you need to hear."

The phone went silent on his end, for so long that Ansinette regretted not hanging up. Finally, he said, "I didn't know I hurt you so bad. I think about how I did you wrong all the time, but I didn't know you were so affected by it. I was hoping you could find it in your heart to forgive me. Some of the best times of my life were spent with you and the boys."

"I can't tell. You never come by to see them. You haven't picked them up for a weekend in months."

Devon let out a long sigh. Through the phone Ansinette could hear a television playing. A crowd cheered in the background. She wondered if what he was watching was important enough to keep him from spending time with his children. "Ansinette. You know how busy I am. I'm a city councilman. I barely have enough time to tie my own shoes, let alone Anthony and David's. Don't I give you money every month? I give you more than the courts would make me pay."

He sent twelve hundred dollars a month. That amount helped tremendously, but money wasn't a substitute for a father. Ansinette's hand curled into a tight fist. He just didn't get it. And If he did get it, he could care less. That level of indifference seemed so much worse. She felt the urge to curse him out, but she couldn't risk losing his financial support. She could survive on her own if she had to. It was possible. The boys would have to relinquish a lot of luxuries. It would be difficult, but she couldn't imagine the drama of taking him to court to force him into paying less money than he was voluntarily paying on his own. If she took him to court, he would still be an absent father. It seemed better to keep playing the game by the rules that kept her in the winner's circle.

Instead of arguing, she said, "You could at least talk to them. They haven't heard your voice in weeks."

"Not now. It's too early in the morning. They're growing boys. They need their rest."

"You called to talk to me? About what?"

"The boys, of course."

His lie unnerved her. "They need a father, Devon. Not a check. They're kids, not a bill. You can't throw money around and expect them to grow up perfectly. It doesn't work that way."

"I want to do better, Ansinette. I've been thinking a lot about that. I'm not working now. The office is closed, and with the state shutdown, there isn't much I can do from home. I've got a bag packed. I'm going to stay at your place during this quarantine lockdown. That way the boys will have me, and you and I can decide if we want to get back together."

Marcus was the first thought in her mind. She glanced at her closed bedroom door and imagined him curled up in his sleeping bag. "That's not happening, Devon. I can't risk you coming in here and spreading a disease."

"I don't have the virus."

"You don't know that. On the news, Dr. Fauci said that it has a fourteen-day incubation period. You could kill us all. Nope. Can't let that happen. It's best if you stay home."

Devon went quiet for a long time. "Ansinette. You're

confusing me. You just told me how bad the boys needed me."

"Don't try and turn this around on me. You didn't hear a word I said. You heard what you wanted to hear. You could have come over and seen the boys any time you wanted to before and you chose not to. Now we're on lockdown. You can't come over. End of discussion."

"Don't you want me to drop off the check? I've got it right here."

"Put it in the mail like you always do."

"Ansinette, not this time! If I don't come over, you may never see another check again."

"You son of a bitch."

"Call me what you want, but I know what you need. You've been alone for how long? Almost a year? Have you dated? No. Remember the last time I came over? I had you crawling up the walls. You need me in your life."

David burst in the bedroom and shouted, "Mama! Where's the toolbox? Marcus is hanging a flat screen on the wall in the living room. He needs a screwdriver."

Ansinette pinched the bridge of her nose, knowing what was coming. Devon asked, "Who's Marcus?"

"Devon, I have to go."

"No," he commanded. "Not until you tell me who . . . "

"Ask that redheaded white girl that Robin saw you hugged up at the mall with the other day. See if she'll let you stay with her." His end of the phone went silent.

She hung up and tossed the phone on the bed. It rang less than five seconds later. David looked at the phone. "Is that my dad?"

Ansinette stared at the phone too. "Yes. But he ain't

talking about nothing. Let me get dressed. I'll be out in a minute."

When David walked out, she thought about dressing but decided against it. Marcus had been living in her home for three days. He'd seen her at her worse already. Even at six a.m. with her hair flat and her eyes sleepy. She brushed her teeth, washed her face, and threw on a pink silk bathrobe before stepping out to start her day.

Marcus had already found the toolbox and was hanging the huge flat screen television on the wall when she entered the living room. Anthony and David stood nearby with equally huge smiles plastered across their little faces.

"That's not our TV," she exclaimed.

Marcus adjusted the box a little and then stepped back. "I know. It's mine. The boys didn't have one in their bedroom, so I got mine out of storage. This way they can play video games in their bedroom and you can watch TV out here."

Anthony hurried to her side. "He gave us his PlayStation Four, Mama. And like fifty games."

David ran up beside him. "It's like Kwanzaa all over again!"

Marcus smiled her way. "I never played it anyway. It was collecting dust."

Ansinette met Marcus' eyes from across the room. No smile adorned her face. "You went out?" she asked.

"To the storage unit. I never saw a soul. I even showered and threw my clothes in the washing machine when I got back."

She wanted to complain. He'd just done the most

mannish bullshit anybody could think of, like going out unprotected in the freaking apocalypse to get a damn TV and PlayStation. But the gesture was so sweet that all she could think to say was, "As long as you were safe about it. I guess it's okay."

Anthony and David hugged her waist then ran off to their bedroom, slamming the door behind them.

Ansinette looked at the television that took up most of her wall space. "That's a big ass TV."

Marcus nodded. "Seventy-two inches."

"And you're going to leave it here when you find a new place?"

"I have another one. I bought them on sale. I had one in the living room and one in my bedroom. I never used the one in my bedroom. I only slept there. Besides, it's the least I could do. You opened your home to me without asking for anything in return." He waited for her to reply. She crossed her arms instead. "You look pissed." Still, she stood there. "Okay. Maybe I should have asked you first."

"Maybe?"

"I . . . Ansinette, it was supposed to be a surprise."

"Oh, I'm surprised."

"I didn't mean to upset you."

She moved inside the room, closer to him. "I'm not upset, but it's obvious that you don't have children. I can't take something away once you've given it to them. You put me in a position where I can't say no, Marcus. Please ask me before doing something like that again. Give me a chance to be the mother. If I give them something, it's because they deserve it."

Marcus pursed his lips. "I didn't think about it like that."

They stood still for a moment, neither knowing how to break the silence. Ansinette wasn't angry. She thought bringing the TV was a great idea, but he needed to know that she was the captain of this ship, not him. Yet she couldn't stand to see him averting his eyes, looking sheepish before her. She smiled inside at his discomfort, though her lips did not.

She took a moment to really look at him. Of course she had seen him before, but her busy life blinded her from seeing who he truly was. He stood at an average height. Not quite six feet tall, but a few inches taller than her. He was muscular without looking bulky. His tight biceps bulged in a useful way, not for show. His skin was the color of coffee, doused with a healthy shot of French Vanilla cream. She'd never seen his bald head stubbly or his short beard unkempt. His face was handsome, but not extraordinarily so. He was a well put together man. Imperfect like anyone else. As she appraised him, she told herself that there was nothing special about him, that he was as human as the next man, but she wasn't convinced. The few days they had spent together let her know that he was well above average.

"Well," she began. "We might as well watch a movie. Since you brought this nice television."

Marcus grinned at her signal of surrender. She showed her feminine weakness, but she didn't care. She hadn't seen her boys smile as much in a long while. She needed Marcus to know that she was pleased with his actions, even if he had acted impulsively.

They sat on the couch. Before turning on the television, he asked. "Do you want donuts?

I stopped by Krispy Kreme on the way back. The boys have their own box in their room."

Ansinette raised a concerned eyebrow. "You went

where?"

"They are only open part time. Crazy. Did I forget to mention that?"

"You did." She smirked. "But I will admit . . . I'd love a donut. Tell me you bought a Bavarian cream."

He licked his lips. "I bought two."

Ansinette bit her lip to suppress another smile as he stood and headed to the kitchen. She inhaled the manly scent left in his wake. Her nipples stiffened. Her legs clamped tight to conceal the warmth spreading throughout her thighs. She closed her eyes and thought of his face, wishing he had not left to go to the kitchen. Just being away from him for that long made her feel empty inside. She wanted him to come on to her. That would be confirmation that he felt the same way, but what would she do then? She couldn't take him to her bedroom. Her sons were home. Well . . . she could if they were in their room playing video games. She shook the thought away. What was she thinking? She barely knew him.

"Coffee?" He called from the kitchen. "I made a pot before I left."

"Milk," she replied.

Her palms rubbed stripes over her thighs. She admitted to herself that she liked him. That was a milestone. But she needed to know more. Sure, they had spoken, yet there was so much about him that she didn't know. She hadn't known that he worked in a meat packing plant until he told her the other day. She realized that the talks they'd had before were superficial and bland. Was she a mystery to him too? He didn't act like any other man who had been attracted to her before. Her past flings were like sharks sniffing blood in the water when they suspected she had feelings for them.

Marcus treated her more as a friend than a potential lover. He respected her boundaries. His chivalry should have impressed her, instead it frightened her to death. She needed him to be more forward, if only because she would never open the door herself. If he liked her, he should show it.

Marcus returned carrying a plate stacked with a pyramid of assorted donuts and two glasses of milk. His chocolate. He placed the plate and drinks on the table, then sat beside her.

Ansinette spied the donuts with suspicious eyes. "I'm only having one."

Marcus reached for the dark chocolate glazed donut. "What are you talking about? I brought the rest for me."

Her smile lit the room as she punched him in the arm. "Oh, you . . ."

He sank his teeth into the donut.

Ansinette watched him, her smile dissipating. "Where are you from? You don't have a North Carolina accent." She picked up a donut and nibbled a corner like a lady, not a famished cretin.

Marcus swallowed. "California. I spent my early years in Pasadena. My mom moved us out here when I was thirteen, because my grandmother was sick. She held on for a little bit, but then she passed. My mom moved back west four years ago."

Ansinette bit her Bavarian cream. "Us?"

"Me and my brother Darryl."

"I didn't know you had a brother."

Marcus bit his donut and chewed slowly before answering. "I don't talk to him much. He's locked up. Been in there six years now."

Ansinette swallowed hard, wishing she hadn't asked. She wanted to know more, but she didn't want to seem nosy. Marcus continued on without prodding. "My dad left us when we were young. I remember a face with a thick mustache. That's it. Whenever I think of him, I see Lionel from *Sanford and Son*. That's my image of a father. Looking like a big dummy. My mom never dated anybody else."

Ansinette assumed that his mother had seen other men but kept her relationships a secret. Marcus couldn't know how hard it was for a single mother to raise two boys without a man in the house. How do you introduce a father figure? The boys would bond with him, but what would happen if the loving relationship went sour? The man couldn't just leave the mother. He'd have to leave the whole family. The boys would experience the hurt of losing a dad all over again. It seemed better to have no man at all.

Marcus turned to her. "What about your family. I know you have a sister. Robin, right?"

"You met her."

"She tried to lure me into her car with a bottle of Hennessey and a box of condoms."

Ansinette laughed. "She, uh . . . she's a wild one. But she's all I have. My mother divorced my stepfather after I left for college, and she died shortly after. My father was never there either. So we've got that in common."

He nodded along. "What do you do for a living? Must be important."

"I'm a project manager for Heritage Systems."

"The tech company? You guys produce software for medical supply companies, right?"

Ansinette nodded. "You know Heritage?"

"I was going to submit my resume."

Ansinette frowned. "You'd need a college degree."

Marcus blinked her way. "What makes you think I don't have a college degree?"

"I don't know," she said, suddenly on the defense. "You work at a meat plant. You need a degree for that?"

"I have a degree," Marcus declared.

Ansinette didn't want to sound as if she didn't believe him, but she was truly surprised.

"Where from?"

"For your information, I went to LSU right out of high school. I had to leave during my junior year. I went back two years ago. I just finished my B.A. in Business Administration this past fall. I was supposed to walk the stage this summer. I don't know how that'll turn out now. COVID has killed everything."

Ansinette couldn't think of an adequate reply. "I had no idea."

"I don't go around telling everybody that. I messed up a good opportunity when I was a kid. I finished what I started. That's all. I had an interview with Panda last week."

"The investment firm?"

Marcus nodded. "I want to be a project manager too. I hoped they would have responded by now. With the pandemic, there's no telling what'll happen."

"You'll get it," she said to encourage him. "If they see half of what I see in you, you'll have a job soon."

She watched him smile again. Ansinette thought that all new relationships began the same way. Each encounter seemed new. A relationship's young days were filled with kind words, encouragement, and smiling faces. She wondered if a couple ever existed that kept those good feelings eternally? If a relationship could progress upon the positive foundation of a new bond, love would always be a miraculous thing. She wasn't sure if that kind of perfection existed. She asked, "Why did you leave college the first time? Obviously, you're smart enough to have finished."

Marcus looked away. His smile metamorphosed into a tight-lipped grimace. Whatever memory she forced him to recall drew crow's feet at the corners of his eyes. He turned back to tell her, "I went to prison."

All Ansinette could think to say was, "Damn."

"I don't mind telling you about it," he continued. "But not now."

She searched his eyes and wasn't sure what she saw. "Okay. We'll talk about it later."

Marcus sat back on the couch and stared off into space, the donuts and the pleasantries they once shared now lie spoiled with the rotten past.

Ansinette reached for the remote control. "Let's watch some Netflix. I've been dying to see *Queen and Slim*."

She searched for the movie, but the whole time she was thinking. *I can't believe I let a felon sleep in my house. And with my kids!*

Five

MARCUS

HE ENTERED THE HOTEL ROOM wearing a black tuxedo and a white phantom of the opera mask. She was already in bed wearing a negligee that looked as pure as milk against her chocolate skin. She lay on her side, her plump ass beckoning him. Marcus shed his jacket, dropping it to the floor as he walked to her. She climbed to her hands and knees to meet him at the edge of the bed. Her fingers fumbled with his belt as he unbuttoned the shirt, baring his bulging chest and chiseled abs.

    He yanked off his bow tie just as she loosened his fly. The pants slid down to a puddle at his ankles. She smiled up at him through slippery lips slick with strawberry gloss. He didn't care about kissing. He only felt an animalistic hunger consuming him. He stood panting, his dick solid and hot in her palm. She peered up as she stroked the length of him and flicked the tip of his manhood with her tongue. The sensation made his knees go weak. She grinned up at him as her hand glided up and down his shaft. Breath caught in his lungs when she swallowed him whole.

He could do nothing but mutter, "Damn. Ansinette . . . " as she sucked him.

Marcus awoke with a start as his eyes adjusted to the darkness. The Netflix movie selection screen provided the only dim light illuminating the shadowy living room. He squinted and made out Anthony and David curled up under superhero blankets on the floor. David cradled his NFL football close to his chest. Marcus vaguely remembered spending the day binging on movies. They had watched so many that he couldn't recall a single title. And such was the life of a family on lockdown during the pandemic. They weren't exactly family, but he began to think of them as a family. They had spent so much time together. If not family, how else could he describe their relationship?

He laid his head back on the couch. Snatches of the dream invaded his thoughts in hazy images of passion and desire. Her lips had been wrapped around his penis. Marcus rubbed sleep from his eyes and whispered to himself, "I gotta stop having these dreams."

He looked down. Ansinette's entire body was splayed on top of his. Her head rested heavily on his chest above his heart. He didn't remember how they had ended up in that position, but he needed to get out of it, because his dream still had him rock hard. He tried to adjust. His dick felt wedged into something tight and he couldn't slide it loose by inching his body away. The more he tried to untangle himself, the firmer the grip felt. He couldn't see how their bodies were intertwined in the darkness. He didn't want to wake her—could not wake her—and if she happened to awake, he didn't want his penis stabbing her belly to be the first sensation she felt. His hand slithered between them and found her fist clamped firmly on the shaft of his erect penis through the front of his sweatpants.

He whispered, "Shit."

His entire body stiffened as he debated on what to do. He tried to pry her fingers off but she held on with the grip of death. He tugged at her wrist.

Ansinette shifted and squeezed him harder. "Oh, Marcus . . . " she mumbled and settled into him a little closer.

Marcus stiffened. After a few seconds, he tried to pull her fingers away again. "Please, please, please let me go, baby." he prayed. Her fingers slacked up enough for him to slide his penis out. Her hand crept up his body to his chest. She snuggled against him like a teddy bear in a child's grasp.

Marcus breathed a sigh of relief as he adjusted to pull his erection completely free of her body. Something told him to ease from beneath her, but he didn't listen to that soft voice of reason. He had always been cautious with women. He acted as a gentleman. He treated them with respect and gave them space. He never pressured them to like him. He placed his own desires on the back bumper. Timidity wouldn't work with Ansinette. He wanted her more than any woman he had ever wanted in his life. He wouldn't be aggressive, but he resigned to be up front with her about how he felt. At that moment, he wanted to hold her in his arms, so that's what he did. He wrapped her up and closed his eyes, reveling in the comfort her closeness brought him.

THE VIRUS BROUGHT ME MY FIRST LOVE

ANSINETTE COULDN'T BELIEVE she had Marcus right where she wanted him. He lay on his back naked. She straddled his lap, her bare breasts smashed against his chest. His hands cupped the bottom of her wide ass. She was so wet that he could water ski in her pussy. But he wasn't inside of her, yet. His long penis lay wedged between them, rigid against their bellies. Her hips danced in a circle as she grinded her clitoris against the shaft of his dick. It wasn't that she didn't want him inside of her. She wanted to enjoy the sensation of touching him—the sensation of being trapped in his clutch. Somehow that seemed enough. At times, intimacy gave a woman more pleasure than intercourse. At times. Not always.

His finger slid closer to her sweet spot, then pressed inside. A soft gasp escaped her as he plunged deeper to stir her middle. She could have came right then. His tongue swirled in her mouth, making her tongue dizzy with delight.

That was it. She had to have him.

Ansinette raised up and tucked him inside of her. The orgasm began immediately. Every inch that he sank deeper into her racked her body with another convulsion that she savored.

"Marcus!" She cried out.

Hearing her own voice awakened her. Ansinette's eyes shot open. The dream had been so real that her mouth crept open with the remnants of the orgasm that had begun in her sleep. Her thighs clamped around Marcus' knee. She didn't dare move as the pleasure overwhelmed her. When the tidal wave was over, she lay still with her eyes closed, catching her breath.

Ansinette finally opened her eyes. She lay curled on top of Marcus like he was a soft body pillow. His arms cradled her close. Her lips poised inches from his. Her heart beat wildly in her chest. How long had they been spooning? Gently, she looked over and saw Anthony and David dozing on the floor. The morning sky was dark but slowly growing brighter. She couldn't believe it. She'd been laying on him all night. Like some ho. Common sense told her to ease off of him, yet the longer she lay, the less she wanted to move. Common sense never had her body feeling as alive as Marcus' did. She stole another look at his face. His features projected a peace that one could only find in sleep—a peace she admired and wished to share.

As she stared at him, she realized that she felt something for him that she may have never known for another man. Love. It was the strangest thought. How could she love a stranger? Then again, Devon had never made her feel as good. They had lived together for the better part of a decade, and she barely knew him. She learned something disgusting about her babies' daddy with every new day.

Wake up. She thought, as she looked at him. Please wake up and kiss me so that I won't have to wonder how you feel about me. Wake up. But Marcus lay motionless.

She knew that she shouldn't have, but she snuggled in closer and buried her face in the crook of his neck. Her lips brushed him there. His skin felt moist and warm upon contact. She pulled back to admire him. He didn't awake. She leaned in to kiss him, stopped short, then steeled herself and pressed her lips delicately against his. Of course, he didn't respond, and she felt silly doing it, but at least she had mustered the courage. She had done something in the dark that she could never have done in the light. When she pulled away and stared at him, she giggled wishing to do it again but felt fearful that she might like it too much and try something else. It was time to go. She didn't want to do something she would regret later.

Ansinette carefully untangled herself and stood. She crept to the hallway toward her room and stopped, then turned back to whisper, "Sweet dreams," before going to bed.

THE NEXT TIME MARCUS AWOKE the sun beamed in through the living room windows. The tantalizing scent of pancakes hung thick in the air. Aside from a gentle clank in the kitchen, the apartment was quiet. The boys no longer slept on the floor. The television was off. He sat up and peered over the back of the couch. Ansinette scraped a skillet with a spatula to flip a pancake. She wore gray yoga pants and a white tank top. The sight of her curves first thing in the morning had Marcus wishing she was his wife. He wondered how she felt about awakening in his arms.

He stood and walked near, but not too close. He hadn't brushed his teeth, and he didn't want to scare her off. He slid into a chair at the dining room table. "Good morning."

She turned enough for him to see her smile. "Good morning to you. Sleep well?"

His heart fluttered at the memory of holding her in the

night. "I slept well. You?"

"Okay, I guess," she replied. "It was a little chilly in my room last night. Other than that, I was alright."

Marcus took a long look at her. "Your room? How did you get in there?"

She shot him a quizzical eyebrow. "I walked. I woke up in bed, and it was cold."

A million questions crossed his mind. She was lying. She knew that she was lying. And she probably knew that he knew she was lying, but what sense would it make to argue with her about it? She lied because she wasn't okay with how they'd slept. That's the only reason he could think of. Putting her on the defense would accomplish nothing. Maybe embarrassment forced her to ignore what happened. He didn't know her well enough to judge. It didn't matter...

Yes, it did matter.

Marcus needed to know that she desired him as much as he desired her. For the life of him, he couldn't understand why women didn't come out and say what they wanted. Why did they insist on playing guessing games?

Instead of challenging her, he asked, "Where are Anthony and David? Playing video games?"

"You know it. I'm leaving it up to you to make sure Anthony finishes his schoolwork. David finished his during their first week out of class. Anthony will procrastinate into inactivity if you let him. Since you brought them that PlayStation, I suggest you stay on his ass to finish his work, or it'll never get done."

He allowed his eyes to linger on her backside for as long as he dared. His gaze crept up to her breasts. He imagined stepping behind her, pressing his body into hers, planting kisses from her shoulders to her lips.

"Marcus!"

He snapped out of it. "Yeah?"

"My eyes are up *here*!"

"I–I was just thinking about checking on the boys before hopping in the shower." The smile she gave him said that she knew otherwise.

"Mmhm. If you say so."

Anthony and David were engrossed in a fierce Madden football game. Both boys were so stuck on the TV that they didn't notice him peeking in the doorway. "Anthony. Make sure you finish your schoolwork, okay?"

Anthony never removed his eyes from the screen. "Yes, sir."

Marcus closed the door and headed to his room.

Later, he kept seeing her face while showering. He imagined her hands soaping his body, caressing his muscles and paying close attention to his pleasure. His erection grew long and hard. He reached down and stroked it a few times but playing with himself in a strange bathroom didn't feel right. He wasn't a sex fiend. When he came to his senses, he reached down and turned off the hot water, allowing the cold, frigid spray to cool him. His erection settled down.

She had lied to him about where she slept. Maybe it was nothing. Maybe she didn't like him. If that were the case, he couldn't walk around her house lusting after her. He yearned to know if she truly cared for him, but he didn't know how to coax it out of her.

He stepped out of the shower more confused than when he had entered. Only after sliding on a pair of gym shorts did he realize that he'd left his clean shirt on his sleeping bag. Damn. He decided that if he hurried to his room she would never know.

Marcus rushed into the hallway with his chest bare. He was two steps from the bathroom door when she emerged from her bedroom.

Seeing him startled her. She pinched her throat in obvious startlement. "Marcus . . . "

"I'm sorry that you caught me like this. I forgot my shirt in my room." He noticed that her eyes were magnetized to his chest. The thought made him smile. "My eyes are up here."

She met his gaze. Her lips parted slightly. "I wasn't ..."

Her eyes dropped to his chest again. He had no idea where she traveled in her mind, but she was lost to him, far away from the reaches of reality. He stepped close and pressed his lips to hers. She resisted at first. Her body jerked from the shock of his boldness, but soon her inhibitions fell away. His wet towel fell at their feet. His arms circled her waist. He shoved her back into the wall then pulled away a bit. She bit her bottom lip and pulled him close again. He kissed her. Ansinette's mouth opened wide, their tongues met in the middle and danced a forbidden dance that only lovers knew.

Her palms rested against his chest, kneading the muscles there. He responded by gripping her ass in both hands. It was softer than he had imagined. He couldn't wait to slide inside, give her what he knew they both needed.

They stood kissing the minutes away. Marcus' hand slipped beneath the waistband of her yoga pants and dove behind her panties to fondle her moist middle. She was steaming and wet for him. His fingers rolled a tight circle around her clitoris. She moaned in his mouth and stiffened against him. He worked his fingers up and down her slick opening. She kissed him harder. He wanted nothing more than to make her orgasm on his hands, on his tongue, and then on his dick.

She pushed him away with a forceful shove.

He opened his arms to grasp her again.

She held him at bay with a stiff arm. "No, no, no, no, no…"

"Ansinette."

She scooted away with her back to the wall and hurried into her bedroom, locking the door behind her.

Six

ANSINETTE

ANSINETTE CALLED ROBIN five times in rapid succession and her sister didn't pick up the damned phone. Ansinette shook her head, "Girl, what are you doing? We're all on quarantine." The next call was a FaceTime. Robin picked up on the third ring. Ansinette hurried to speak before Robin could get out a hello. "I have been calling and calling. What are you doing?"

Robin wouldn't look at the phone. She kept her eyes downcast. Ansinette noticed that her sister's hair sat lopsided. She wore the same pajama top that she'd been wearing for the last three days.

"Robin? What's wrong?"

"I'm sorry, Ansinette, but this quarantine is kicking my ass."

That was the last thing Ansinette wanted to hear. She needed someone to talk to about Marcus. Robin was the only person she had to call. She confronted her sister's sad expression and pushed her problems to the side. "I think David might have some batteries in one of his old toys. I'll see if I can bring them to you."

"It's not that. I found some batteries. But Harold isn't the same. I never thought a vibrator could act like a man."

"What do you mean?"

"He let me down, Ansinette. I'll never be able to look at him the same. Once the trust is gone, so is the love." Robin lifted a bottle to her lips and turned it up.

Ansinette squinted at her phone. "Are you drinking? It's not even two o'clock."

Robin waved her off. "So what? I'm stuck in the house. I'm lonely. I'm sick of watching TV. Tired of surfing the internet. I am bored out of my fucking mind. I need to get drunk. Maybe it'll help Stella get her groove back."

Ansinette wanted to scold Robin for the way she was acting, but the lockdown hadn't been easy on anyone. If Marcus hadn't brought his video game machine over, Anthony and David would have driven her up the wall. At least she had Marcus to keep her company. She may have felt awkward with the emotions his presence pulled out of her, but she wasn't bored. Not at all.

Robin said, "You don't look so good yourself."

Now that Ansinette knew how Robin was feeling, complaining about her problems seemed inappropriate. "It's not important."

"Come on, Ansinette. You never call unless it's important. You're a texter, not a caller. Let me find out there's trouble in paradise."

Ansinette took notice of the way Robin perked up. Boredom had her grasping for any salacious conversation. Robin's question summoned the memory of Marcus' lips on hers. She closed her eyes for a second and could smell him, fresh out of the shower, as if he stood before her.

"He kissed me," she whispered, then glanced at her closed bedroom door in fear of him pressed against it and listening on the other side. She wouldn't dare recount how she had kissed him as he slept. She wasn't ready to divulge anything like that. "He pressed me against the wall and kissed me."

The first smile tugged at the corners of Robin's lips. "Was it good?"

Ansinette rolled her eyes. "Girl, yes."

Robin squealed her delight. "I want to know everything. Did his breath stink? Had he shaved? Were his teeth too big? Did he suck your tongue?"

Ansinette described their encounter detail for detail, from the time she went into her bedroom to check her emails for work to the instant she had left him panting in the hallway with his chest heaving like some famished tiger in the jungle, who was watching his prey escape into the thicket. Her nipples stiffened along with her quickening heart. When she closed her eyes, she could feel his biceps cupped in her palm. His handprints were still warm on her backside in spots where he had touched her.

Robin sucked in a breath when Ansinette finished the tale. "He had his fingers all up in there?"

Ansinette quivered at the thought. "I couldn't stop myself. He knew just how to touch me. It was like I was a guitar and his fingers were plucking a slow song of joy and pain between my legs. It was too much. He made me crazy."

"Why did you stop him? Sounds like you wanted to yank him into the room. I would have. Shit, you haven't had a real man in a long time. You deserve some good D."

Ansinette didn't have an answer. She wanted nothing more than to pull him to her bed and let him go to work. She admitted that to herself. If her sons hadn't been in the house, she might have done it. Yet there would come a time when even the boys wouldn't be a good excuse, and she would have to confront her desires. She and Marcus would tear each other apart if they stayed in that apartment together for much longer. That fact hovered over her head and in her heart. She couldn't bring herself to do it while standing in that hallway though. Not then.

She told Robin, "There's still so much that I don't know about him."

"What's not to know? He's fine. He's got a delicious body. He has a nine-to-five. He may be laid off now, but things will get back to normal . . . hopefully soon." Robin paused. A sly smile spread across her lips. "Does he have a big dick?"

"What?"

"His dick. Was it hard when it was touching you?"

Ansinette snorted a laugh. "It felt like a sword rubbing against my thigh."

"Damn!" Robin declared, then took another hit of her liquor. "I need a fucking man. Got me horny and jealous up in here. Tell me he has a fine ass brother somewhere." Ansinette only laughed. Robin went on. "Did you ever see women come to his apartment?"

Ansinette thought about it. "I saw one. She was light-skinned and pretty. Young. She used to come over all the time, but I never spoke to her. I'm sure they were together. I haven't seen her in a couple of months, and he doesn't talk about her."

"That's good," Robin confirmed. "That means they broke up. How old is Marcus anyway?"

"Twenty-nine, I think."

Robin raised an eyebrow. "A younger man. Gotta watch them. They'll hurt you."

"How? Cheating?"

"No," Robin declared. "Stamina. A man under thirty will pump you dry. You didn't know? They never want to stop. Do you remember that boy Roderick that I used to mess with? The one with the cockeye and limp? He used to go all night. Had me wobbling around like a duck-billed platypus in the office the next morning. My boss asked me if I rode a horse to work. I told him, 'shit, I didn't ride one to work, but I rode one last night.'" They both snickered. "I told Roderick that he could only see me on Fridays. I needed two days to recuperate. Too much of a good thing will kill you."

"Robin, it isn't always about sex. I think I really like this one. I've never met anybody like him."

"Well, what's the problem?"

Ansinette paused before confessing, "He said that he's been to prison."

"Is that all? You'll be hard pressed to find a black man who hasn't been locked up, Ansinette. You're lucky he's working and not out there robbing people or selling drugs."

Ansinette hung her head low. "I don't know. I've never dated a—a criminal."

"Stop trying to find something wrong with him. You're sabotaging yourself. Sometimes you have to cut away the rotten parts of an apple to enjoy the rest of it. I tell you what. I'll run a background check on him."

"I could have done that myself."

"You didn't. Let me do it. It'll satisfy your curiosity. I want to see you happy. Besides, you need to know what kind of man has been playing in your coochie. He might turn out to be some kind of freak. You've got me chomping at the bit to find out. What's his last name?"

"Jenkins. Marcus Jenkins."

Robin nodded. "I'll call you back with the tea."

Hours after her phone call with Robin, Ansinette found it difficult to abandon the edge of her bed. She and Marcus had been avoiding each other all day; well, as much as they could in her small apartment which made it worse. He'd been hiding in his room working on his laptop. She'd been in hers doing the same. She had used Zoom to attend a meeting and outlined a report that she'd been neglecting. Those tasks had taken up the morning and most of the afternoon. She saw him in the boys' room playing video games when she left to get a drink, but they didn't speak. They needed to talk. That was evident. They would face each other eventually, and she didn't fear the confrontation. She feared the emotions that may come out of her when the confrontation arrived. She gathered her nerve and left her bedroom.

Marcus sat on the couch watching an old football game with David when she walked out. He looked up. His eyes followed her to the kitchen. Ansinette rummaged through the cabinets for food. They barely had anything to eat. Someone would need to go to the store soon.

Marcus stepped into the kitchen. She faced him. They stared at each other for a moment, each unsure of what to say. Finally, he broke the ice. "I should go to the store. We don't have much to eat."

She nodded. "I'll give you the money and a list."

"Just the list. I'll take care of the groceries."

Ansinette didn't have the heart to protest. She forced herself to meet his eyes, though she wanted to turn away in shame. Why couldn't she just talk to him?

Marcus stepped close and ran his fingers along her forearm. "I'm sorry about this morning. I–I thought you wanted me to—Ansinette, I really care for you. I have for a while now. Maybe you don't like me. That's okay. I needed to tell you how I felt . . . "

"How do you feel?" She blurted.

"Like I've been waiting for you all of my life, and if I don't find out if you're the woman I need, I'll lose my mind. Maybe that's why I moved too quickly."

She wanted to kiss him then. She wanted to feel her body pressed against his, but the timing wasn't right. She peeked in on David. His eyes were locked on the TV. "It's okay, Marcus," she whispered. Ansinette eased in close so they could talk without David hearing. "I like you too. I just–I..."

Marcus rushed to say, "We don't have to do anything, Ansinette. It's not all about sex with me. I want to know who you are. I want to watch your sons grow up. I want to love you . . ."

"Love?" She hacked up an inch. "You barely know me."

"I know enough."

He reached out and rested his hand on her hip. She allowed it. "Marcus. Don't you have other women that you talk to? I used to see some girl going to your place."

"Joy?" He laughed. "I haven't even thought about her in weeks. We haven't been together in months."

Ansinette lowered her eyes. "Yes, but she was beautiful. Much more beautiful than me. I'm not what you like."

His ex, Joy, was light-skinned and trim. She wore tight dresses to broadcast her yellow thighs and round behind. Ansinette cringed each time she saw her exiting her black BMW in a cloud of perfume. Her eyes hid behind expensive, oversized sunglasses.

Marcus held both of Ansinette's hands in his and forced her to look at him. "You don't have to worry about Joy."

"Why not? If not her, some other pretty little light-skinned thing will get your attention, and then what will happen to me?"

She felt the tears only after one dribbled from her chin.

"You are beautiful, Ansinette. I don't know who convinced you that you aren't. You don't have to look like Joy to be pretty. She spent a lot of money to make herself look better than she really did. You have beautiful skin." He stroked her arm. "Soft lips. A lovely body. All of that attracts me to you, but what attracts me most is your mind. I've learned so much about you in the last few days. Feels like I've known you my whole life. And you accept me for who I am. Joy looked down on me because I didn't make that much money. She was all about the cars and clothes. I couldn't afford that stuff, and if I could have, I still wouldn't want them. Those things don't make a person happy. How your heart communicates with mine brings me happiness. Give me a chance. I'll show you."

Ansinette's gaze bounced back and forth between his eyes. She wanted to believe him, but Devon had said most of those things on numerous occasions. It wasn't fair to think

Marcus would treat her the same way, but she wasn't sure. "I just left a bad relationship, Marcus. That's not your fault, but it makes it hard for me to trust people. I don't know if I'm ready for this. I was fine being single. Then you came along and made me feel things I have never felt before. We haven't even been out on a date."

"We can't go out now. Everything looks like its closed."

She almost smiled. "I know. But that isn't the point. I like you. I'm not sure what I want." She backed away. "Give me time."

Marcus took her place leaning against the stove. She hated seeing the sadness in his eyes, yet she didn't know what else to do.

He looked at the floor and muttered, "Okay."

Seven

MARCUS

HE DROVE THROUGH THE GHOST TOWN he had once known as Raleigh, North Carolina. Before leaving the apartment, he had expected to see the world drenched in pandemonium. Scenes of rioters that he'd seen on the news crossed his mind. Instead he found vacant parking lots and deserted streets. Once bustling storefronts in strip malls sat dormant with inner shadows blanketing lifeless products collecting dust on display. No cars stood at intersections allowing him to drive through red lights, when he would have been stopped for fifteen minutes before. He found three epicenters where masses congregated: drive-thrus at fast food restaurants, gas stations, and grocery stores.

Many stores were closed. Their parking lots lay as lifeless as graveyards with empty spaces outlining plots where prosperity now perished. He drove through three towns before finding a Food Lion open in Apex, and they only offered curbside assistance. Ansinette wrote out a mile-long list and waited in his truck for ninety minutes. The store clerk returned with half of the items on his list. He wanted to complain, but he looked in his rearview mirror and found it impossible to count the line of cars snaking behind him. *Everyone needs food*, he thought. He drove off determined to find another open store.

At a Costco in Fuquay-Varina, he found the items he needed, and a store clerk told him that a food supplier was holding a chicken sale at the state fairgrounds in Raleigh. The chicken had been frozen in forty-pound boxes for restaurants that were not in business during the pandemic. Sellers were forced to peddle the chicken from the back of a semi-truck to ordinary citizens at a discount. Marcus drove as fast as he could to make it back to Raleigh. He found another train of cars. This time he made up the caboose. The sky was painted a dark purple by the time he pulled up to the back of the truck. A fat white guy waddled to his window. "You're in luck. We've got one forty-pound box of boneless, skinless breasts for seventy dollars." Marcus looked in his wallet. He had fifty-six in cash. The white guy shrugged. "We'll take it. We had a good day."

He made it to the apartment around seven. David walked into the kitchen as he stocked the refrigerator. "Where's your mom?"

David walked over to help him unload the groceries. "Sleeping. She was on the phone for a long time. I guess she was tired."

Marcus couldn't blame her. He'd been gone for half the day. He glanced over at the kitchen table. Anthony's books were scattered on its surface, but it didn't look like he'd done anything. "Where's your brother?"

David lugged a gallon of milk to the refrigerator. "Playing Assassin's Creed."

"Has he been playing games all day?"

David nodded. "He hasn't left the room except to pee."

Marcus looked over at the dining room table again. "David, Tell your brother I'd like to speak to him."

Anthony dragged into the kitchen five minutes later looking tired and annoyed. He came alone. "What's up, Marcus?"

Marcus had just finished putting everything away. He'd left out the chicken, rice, and broccoli. "Why haven't you been doing your schoolwork? Don't you have a report to do on Genghis Khan?"

Anthony's eyes dropped to the linoleum floor. "It's pass/fail anyway. I've done enough to pass."

"That's not the point, Anthony. I thought you liked learning about Genghis."

"I did." Anthony admitted. "But once you know everything about him, what else is there?"

Many of the women Marcus dated in the past had small children. Although, he had never been met with such childhood logic. He walked to the dining room table and pulled out two chairs. "Sit down, Anthony." Anthony sat, but he wouldn't meet Marcus' gaze. "There's always something to learn. It is impossible to know everything. Your teachers assign you work so they can know how well you process information. Think of it as climbing stairs. One teacher prepares you for what the next will teach."

Marcus wanted to explain that he had been just like Anthony. Procrastination was a way of life for him as a kid.

Most of his days were spent playing basketball or football, not in a book. The hardest lesson he learned in life was not only Work Hard but you have to Play even Harder. This fact didn't dawn on him until he found himself overwhelmed during his freshman year in college. He struggled to write research papers because he had not mastered the fundamentals of writing. Other students were light years ahead of him. Instead of working harder to catch up, he rebelled and gave up on himself. Something he now regretted.

"I'm not as smart as the other kids," Anthony said.

Marcus crossed his arms. "Why do you say that?"

"I don't know. It doesn't take them as long to understand stuff. I'm stupid."

Something like a fist squeezed Marcus' heart. He remembered saying the same thing to his mother decades ago. It was a stock statement that all boys stowed away in a bag of excuses, employed to extract sympathy and compassion. When Marcus said something like that, he hoped his mother would feel sorry for him and let him be. He was lucky she hadn't. Even though he never did well in school, Betty ensured that he did something. That minimal effort kept his grades level. Football carried him further than his mind did, but Betty never let him give up.

He met Anthony's eyes. "Smart people aren't smart because they were born smart. They work for it. They don't make excuses. They find a way to make it work." Marcus noticed that the more he spoke, the more sheepish Anthony looked. He didn't want the boy to think he was talking down to him. Marcus tried to give him the talk he never heard from a man. "You might find that your assignments aren't as hard as you think. All you have to do is sit down and do them.

You'll be finished before you know it."

"That's the hard part," Anthony admitted. "I don't want to do it."

"You think I like going to work?" Marcus smiled.

"You don't understand, Marcus. Every time I try to do something, it turns out wrong. I fail at everything."

Marcus slapped the table. "That's great."

Anthony stared at him, dumbfounded. "It is?"

"Everybody fails. But when you get something wrong, it gives you a chance to learn from your mistakes and improve on them. Michael Jordan was cut from his high school basketball team. But he worked hard all that year. The next time he tried out, the coach put him on as a starter."

Anthony blinked. "Who's Michael Jordan?"

"Come on, man. I'm not that old. I was a kid when he was about to retire . . . "

"Is he the guy that makes the shoes?" Marcus nodded. Anthony continued, "I didn't know he played basketball."

Marcus had to laugh. "He was the greatest player that ever lived. But he's not the only great person who failed at something. Everybody fails, kid. Life is hard. You need to dig down deep and find a way to succeed. First, you have to put in the work."

Anthony held Marcus' gaze. "I'll try."

"Don't try, Anthony. Do it. I'll help you."

Anthony looked away. Marcus expected the boy to say something defiant. Instead, tears sprouted from the corners of his eyes and ran in rivers down his cheeks. He made no move to wipe them. He sat there, bathed in grief, as if they didn't exist. Marcus stood and pulled the boy to him.

"I'm sorry, Anthony. I didn't mean to upset you. I don't want you to make the same mistakes I made growing up. If a man had been around to teach me, it would have saved me and my brother a lot of trouble."

"You weren't too hard on me," Anthony replied, finally pulling himself together.

"Then what is it?"

Anthony pulled away. "Nothing."

Marcus took his seat again so they could be eye to eye. "If you don't want to tell me, I understand."

"I wish you were my dad," Anthony declared.

Of all the things Marcus expected to hear, that wasn't one of them. He had thought about having kids, but getting his own life in order proved challenging enough. Being a father dropped to the bottom of his *to do* list long ago. A part of him didn't think he could be a good father. He never had an example.

"Why would you say that, Anthony?"

A fresh wave of tears washed Anthony's face. "Because you talk to me. You spend time with me. My dad . . . he doesn't care about us. He doesn't call. He doesn't come by. Even when he lived with us, he was always working. Whole days would go by without him saying a word to me. He hates us."

Anthony's fingers curled into fists at his sides. His eyes changed from hurtful to murderous in an instant. Marcus grabbed him again. This time he squeezed Anthony until tears ran rampant from his own eyes and he had to shut them to stop crying. He embraced him until he was transported back to a small house in California, and he was that angry boy with low self-esteem. As a fatherless child, he knew how a boy's anguish could fester and turn into rage if ignored or misunderstood. He wondered how many black boys grew into killers because their fathers were absent. How many thought that running the streets was something a man was supposed to do because they had no guidance? He had known thousands. They filled the cells of prisons in the United States. They grew up unbalanced and immature. Violence in prison became the example of masculinity, not compassion and fatherhood. Reading books about slavery taught him that such a chain will continue. There would always be a black, fatherless child somewhere, but he would be damned to see it happen to Anthony, whether he was with Ansinette or not.

Marcus refused to make excuses for Anthony's father. He didn't know the situation, and he didn't want to pass judgement. He wouldn't bad mouth him either. When both of their tears had dried, Marcus sank to his knees. He said, "My dad left me too. I never got over it. My big brother went crazy, but I was lucky, because I played football. Half a dozen coaches saw something in me and wouldn't let me fail. Through them I learned how a man was supposed to act."

Anthony lowered his gaze. "I don't have anybody to do that for me."

"You have me." Anthony raised his eyes. Marcus smiled at the boy's hope. He could feel it. "I'll always be here for you. I know that we're just getting to know each other, but we're friends now. I won't let you down."

"Yeah, but my mom said that you don't live across the hall anymore. That's why you have to stay with us until the pandemic is over. You might move too far away."

Marcus looked at him. "I have a truck. I'm only a phone call away."

Anthony thought about that. "Why don't you just ask my mom if you can be her boyfriend? Then you could live with us forever."

Marcus laughed because he was beginning to like the mind of a child. "It's not that simple."

"Yes, it is. I do it all the time. I have a million girlfriends at school. And she likes you. I heard her talking on the phone to my Aunt Robin while you were gone."

"You eavesdropped on your mom?"

"They were talking loud. You should have heard the stuff they said about you. I had to close my door because it was so nasty. I'm not supposed to watch movies that use words they were saying."

Marcus was all ears. "What did they say?"

"'I can't repeat it."

"Tell me what you can repeat. You're killing me here, Anthony."

Anthony lost his nerve. "I don't know. You might tell my mom."

"What? I want to see her happy. Maybe what you tell me can help me do that."

Anthony chewed his lip, then whispered, "She said that she wished you two had went out on a date before she let you move in. She wanted to know if y'all had biology or something."

"Chemistry?"

"Yeah, that's it."

"Robin said that she should tell you how she felt, but my mom thought you might take advantage of her if she did. I think she's scared of you."

Marcus grit his teeth so hard his jaw hurt. "She's not afraid of me. She's afraid of how she feels."

"She doesn't believe in herself," Anthony decided. "Like you said about me. She needs somebody to give her confidence."

"I think you're right."

"They were talking about something else, but I don't know if I should tell you . . ."

Marcus rested a hand on his shoulder. "You can trust me."

Anthony gulped. "They were talking about your—your privates."

"You're right. You should not repeat that."

They both laughed, but Anthony had no idea how he had helped Marcus. If they weren't on lockdown, he would take her out. All he needed was to show her a good time. But they were on lockdown, and nothing was open. He looked around the kitchen. *What can I do?* He thought. The chicken sat thawing on the counter.

He turned to Anthony. "How does your mom like her chicken?"

Eight

ANSINETTE

THE CLOCK READ SEVEN-FORTY when she awoke. She lay in bed staring up at the ceiling not believing that she had slept the whole day away. Her phone showed eleven missed calls. Ten from Devon. One from Robin. She would call Robin back soon. Not Devon. Devon had carved out a permanent spot on her shit list. Who did he think he was telling her what to do? He lost that right when he decided to lay down with other women during their relationship.

Thinking of her past with Devon, lowered her spirits even more. How could she have been such a fool? Devon never cared for her. When they were together, he treated her like shit because she allowed it. Twelve years. He never once asked her to marry him. She brought it up of course, and he diverted the conversation before giving a definitive answer.

Slivers of the dark blue sky outside peeked back at her. She couldn't think of a single moment of happiness with Devon. Every day brought drama. Marcus would never treat her that way. He proved his loyalty long before she admitted to herself that she liked him. Every day with him brought the promise of something new.

Her phone chimed. It was a text from Robin. The message was short: *found out some info on your boy*. A link to a website glowed in blue at the bottom. It would be information about Marcus' criminal past. Ansinette's finger hovered over the link. Debating whether or not to push it weighed heavily on her heart. Did she really want to know? Her reluctance derived from the fear that she would find out about some heinous crime and be compelled to dislike him. The truth may tarnish his character in unforgivable ways. She wouldn't be able to look at him the same if he'd done something crazy.

Yet she had to know the true identity of the man living in her house.

She clicked the link.

It took her to WRAL's news archive. Right away, Ansinette spotted a still video of Marcus' mugshot. The caption above the video read, "Rapist Released After Only 5 Years in Prison." The phone trembled in her hand. She needed to click the video. Her finger remained poised above it. She tossed the phone on the bed. She stood up to pace back and forth while casting sidelong glances at the still image on the screen. Marcus—sweet, handsome Marcus—a rapist? Ansinette thought back to their moment in the hallway. At first his aggression turned her on. What woman didn't want a man to take control and make her feel helpless to his charms?

The mannish way he'd fondled her ass told her that he would be a beast in the bedroom. His probing fingers hadn't been rough. His touch was tender, loving. He knew just how to touch her. During that moment, she wanted him. If Anthony and David hadn't been home, she would have dropped her pants right there. He stopped when she said "no." But knowing what she knew now had her questioning his aggression. Could he have raped her?

She looked at the phone again. Thinking in circles did her no favors. All she needed to do was click on the video. The answers she sought may be revealed in the news report. She hugged herself while debating, then decided against it. She left the phone on her bed as she headed to the shower, thinking that it was going to be a long night and she needed to clear her head.

The steamy water made Ansinette think of him even more. She tried to force the passionate thoughts from her mind, but visions of Marcus plagued her. She closed her eyes and saw him with no shirt. She remembered how her hands massaged his bulging biceps. She had felt small in his arms, swallowed by his masculinity. The hot shower spray tingled her nipples. Every drop of water that hit her clitoris sent a spark through her body. A man had never made Ansinette feel the way Marcus did. Submitting to him meant relinquishing her independence.

Sexually, she wouldn't stop him from doing anything that he wanted. Even thoughts of him drove her insane. She touched herself to arousal, then stopped. No man should have that type of power over a woman. Especially when she had questions about his past.

Ansinette climbed out of the shower horny and

frustrated. She dried off and put on a robe, then stared in the mirror knowing that she couldn't hide in her room forever. In the reflection, she spotted something white spread across her bed behind her. *What is that?*

She walked back into the bedroom. A white dress that she hadn't worn since her clubbing days lay draped neatly across her bedspread. It had thin shoulder straps, a plunging neckline, and a skirt that flowered out high above her knees. A card envelope rested beside the dress. Ansinette opened the envelope. She recognized her son David's scrawl. He had written. "You Are Invited to Dinner."

Dinner?

Ansinette opened her bedroom door. "David!"

The boy emerged from the living room wearing his good Sunday suit and dress shoes. He grinned up at her. "Yes, Mama?"

She fingered his clothes. "Boy, what are you wearing . . . and why have you been rummaging through my closet? What have I told you about going through my things?"

David kept on smiling. "I had to find you something to wear. Hurry up and get dressed. Dinner is almost ready." He turned and skipped back down the hall toward the living room.

Ansinette stood in her doorway frowning. She sniffed the air. Fried chicken. Cheese. Her growling belly reminded her that she hadn't eaten a thing. She vaguely remembered sending Marcus to the store. She closed the door.

The dress seemed to glow beneath a spotlight with a halo above it. She walked over slowly, wondering what she was getting herself into. If the boys liked him, that was one hurdle she wouldn't have to worry about stumbling over. She sat on the edge of her bed, knowing a candlelit dinner awaited. Tears accompanied the slow smile that spread across her lips. Beside the dress, lay her phone. The screen was dark, but she knew one touch would bring it back to life and shatter the happiness she desired to find with Marcus. How did she get in this position?

She couldn't disappoint her boys. Obviously, they had been working to please her. Sorrow commandeered much of their life. Maybe it would please them to see her happy; if she could feel happy. Ansinette dressed, donning white low-tops and a radiant smile as her most comely accessory.

The apartment was dimly lit when she entered. The place was spotless. Soft music played from a YouTube channel on TV. The dining room table was covered with the burgundy tablecloth she usually pulled out for Thanksgiving. Fresh flowers protruded from a vase—flowers that she recognized from the small garden in front of the apartment complex's clubhouse. Anthony wore his best suit as well. The boys stood side by side near the doorway. Both projected stern expressions devoid of a smile.

David held out his arm and gestured to the dining room table. "Right this way, Madame." Ansinette burst out laughing at his performance. *Madame?* She wondered how many times he'd practiced that.

Both boys erupted in a giggling fit. Anthony was the first to straighten up. He slapped David on the shoulder. David shook away his laughter. "Madame." He gestured to a chair at the table.

Ansinette kept on smiling with pride, not ridicule. "Okay." She sat.

Marcus stood in the kitchen, shoveling something onto a

plate. He wore slacks, a dress shirt, and a red tie. Anthony and David hurried to him. Marcus leaned down and whispered something to them. The boys nodded.

Marcus walked to the living room and smiled down on Ansinette. "You look beautiful."

"You do, Mama." David added.

She had no time to jazz up her natural hair the way she wanted to. She'd massaged a dab of moisturizer into her scalp and parted it so that the top swooped to one side. It wasn't perfect, but it would do. She barely brushed on makeup and smeared a smacking of gloss across her lips before hurrying to the delicious scents in the kitchen.

Marcus' eyes never left hers as he sat down. He looked good too, she admitted to herself. For a moment she was transported to their escapade in the hallway. The memory forced her to look away from him so that she wouldn't show her attraction.

She put on a happy face for her sons. "What are we having?"

Anthony said, "Chicken Parmesan. Fettuccini Alfredo. Broccoli."

Ansinette licked her lips involuntarily. "I hope it tastes as good as it sounds."

Marcus smiled. "I hope so too." He peered into the kitchen. "Fellas."

Anthony and David hopped into action. Both boys grabbed a plate of food and carefully walked to the table. David moved rigidly. Ansinette hoped he wouldn't drop the plate from being too cautious. He made it to the table safely and grinned as he slid the plate onto the placemat before her. After the food, the boys went back to the kitchen. Anthony carried a pitcher of blue Kool-Aid. David brought two wine flutes.

Ansinette smiled at the Kool-Aid. "Is that what I think it is?"

David's grin lit the room. "I made it." He leaned in close to her ear. "Six cups of sugar."

Ansinette whispered back. "Just the way I like it. Diabetic coma."

The boys stood back and stared after they finished serving dinner. Marcus said, "Thanks guys. I'll take it from here."

David looked to Ansinette. "If you will excuse us, Madame. We will retire to our room for our own dinner and a night of *Capcom Versus Marvel* on the PlayStation."

Ansinette nodded. "Retire on then." She watched as the boys hurried off to their bedroom. She smiled to Marcus. "Who are those children, and what did you do with mine?"

Marcus laughed, but not for too long. "I wish I had been that smart when I was their age."

"Thank you," she said. "How did you get them to act so well-mannered?"

"Wasn't my idea." He gestured to the food with open arms. "This was all their doing. I just went along with it."

Ansinette was taken aback. "They convinced you to cook dinner and make a date night for me?"

Marcus nodded. Ansinette couldn't believe it. She knew Marcus and the boys had been bonding, but she didn't know they liked Marcus enough to act as matchmakers. She turned around and stared at their closed door in disbelief. She wasn't sure if she should be proud or furious. When she turned back to Marcus, he was still smiling.

THE VIRUS BROUGHT ME MY FIRST LOVE

She looked down at the food. The chicken breast was fried golden brown with juicy tomato sauce and gooey mozzarella cheese oozing down the sides. The fettuccini gleamed in the dim lighting, and the broccoli looked succulent. Her eyes fell on Marcus again. "You did all of this for me?"

"Of course not. I haven't eaten all day either." He smiled. "But it was my pleasure."

"Marcus..."

"It wasn't that much. I cook all the time. I'm honored to cook for you."

Ansinette's smile faded. "Why? We barely know each other..."

"This is how we'll get to know each other. You invite me into your home. I cook dinner for you. We talk. We won't get married tomorrow."

"Married?"

"Like I said," he continued. "Not tomorrow. Someday."

Ansinette picked up her fork and knife, planning to shovel food into her mouth to stop from talking. The man drove her crazy. He was talking about marriage, and the thought pleased her beyond belief. She sliced off a piece of chicken and speared it with her fork.

"Wait," he said.

Ansinette paused with the fork inches from her mouth.

"We have to say grace first."

How could she have forgotten about God?

Marcus bowed his head and closed his eyes. Ansinette did the same as he gave thanks.

"Father God," Marcus began. "Thank you for the life you have given us. Thank you for Ansinette's smart little boys. And thank you for blessing us through this pandemic..." Ansinette opened her eyes to steal a glance at him as he prayed.

She couldn't understand how this man committed a heinous crime like rape. It didn't seem possible.

"And Lord," Marcus continued. "I only ask that you protect us from the coronavirus and see us through this troubled time safely. In Your name, Amen."

Ansinette echoed his, "Amen."

They ate the first few bites in silence. Ansinette's eyes closed with each chew as she savored Marcus' chicken. It tasted better than any chicken she had ever cooked.

He sat expectant. "Do you like it?"

She paused long enough to say, "I love it. Are you good at everything you do?"

Marcus sipped Kool-Aid from his wine glass. "I try to be. I lost a lot of time. When I was in prison, I planned to be a different man when I got out. Most people don't have the opportunities that I had, and I wasted them."

She chewed her food slowly. Each time he offered an answer, it led to another question Ansinette wanted to ask. She had acted shy and humble before. She wanted the truth now.

"What opportunities, Marcus?"

He put his fork down. A pained expression washed over his face. "I had a scholarship to play football at LSU. By junior year I had every team in the NFL ringing my phone to enter the draft. I didn't care about school. I didn't really care about football. I felt that the success I had was owed to me. I made the same mistake a lot of young men make."

Ansinette never stopped eating. It was important for her to project that she was enjoying herself, not probing. "Why didn't you graduate? You made it to junior year. You did something right."

"It wasn't my fault," was all he said.

What wasn't your fault? She wanted to ask. Would that have been too direct? She didn't know. Why couldn't men just come out and say what women wanted to hear? Why did she have to ask? If he liked her as much as he said he did, wouldn't he volunteer the information? Put it all on the table? That would be the honest thing to do.

"Do you dance?" he asked her.

"What?"

"Do you dance? I love this song."

Ansinette tuned her ear to the music. It was Jodeci's "Come and Talk to Me."

She started to say no when Marcus stood and walked to her. He held out his hand. Reluctantly, she stood. Marcus took tentative steps toward her. He wrapped his arms around her waist. She responded by wrapping hers around his neck. Ansinette could tell the power his body held. As they swayed to the music, she had to admit that she didn't fear him. That realization felt important.

She pulled back and looked up into his eyes. She didn't care that he had been to prison or what he went up for. It didn't seem so important right now. Not when her heart was beating thump, thump in her chest.

Marcus smiled at her. "Ansinette? What is it?"

She leaned in and kissed him. Seconds later, she heard giggling from the back hallway. She turned and saw Anthony and David there cracking up.

Nine

ANSINETTE

THE BOYS BEGAN DOZING DURING the middle of *Avengers: Endgame*. After dinner, Marcus decided to watch the entire Avengers trilogy, almost nine hours of movie watching. David held on for as long as he could. He passed out during the first fifteen minutes of the last movie. Anthony lay on his belly, his head propped in his palms. He rebelled exhaustion, jerking himself awake each time his head drooped to sleep.

The dull glow of the television was the only light in the room.

Ansinette still wore her white dress. She had abandoned the shoes long ago. Her bare feet rested curled beneath her on one side of the couch. Marcus slouched beside her. He still wore his pants and shirt. He'd taken off the tie hours ago, soon after Ansinette brought out a bottle of Absolut from her bedroom. She spiked Marcus' Kool-Aid along with hers. The boys never knew. The fruity drink provided the perfect nightcap to their date. They sat close, whispering and sniggering in conspiratorial cackles.

Ansinette learned a lot about Marcus in the few hours that they'd been talking. The liquor loosened their tongues, and she was sure she told him as much about herself. She spoke at length about her childhood with an inattentive mother and a stepfather who only cared about his own vices. Marcus listened without interrupting. His eyes remained unwaveringly on hers soaking up every word. His attention told her that he cared about what she had to say. He only spoke after she had finished a lengthy monologue. She loved that about him. Most men that she knew butted in while she was trying to make a point or they barely paid attention and only cared to speak about the important things in their lives. They were self-centered and arrogant. Marcus gave her the respect she deserved.

In turn, Marcus spoke about his family. She loved that he had a good relationship with his mother. That said a lot about how he treated women. He didn't say much about his brother. Ansinette suspected that his brother had something to do with his past incarceration, but she left that subject alone for the time being, deciding to accept him for who he was, regardless of his past. She couldn't hold him accountable for a situation he had overcome.

Marcus pointed to Anthony, whose head lolled on his shoulders. "He's trying to hold on, look at him." Ansinette snorted as quietly as she could. Anthony collapsed on the floor in a snoozing mass. Marcus held up his drink in a mock toast to Anthony. "A strong soldier."

Ansinette laughed so hard that she almost spilled her drink. "Stop making fun of my son."

"I'm playing," he whispered back. "He's a good kid. He's going to be something special someday."

Ansinette sobered a bit as she watched her son sleep. "If I can ever get him to realize how important his education is."

"He will."

"How do you know?" she asked.

"Because I'm going to help him." Marcus downed the last swallow of his drink.

Ansinette had no answer for that. Their fun-loving banter faded to non-existence. The last thing she needed was some man making empty promises. But strangely, she believed Marcus. He seemed like a man of his word. She hoped he was because Anthony needed a strong man in his life. He needed Marcus.

Marcus glanced at her half-empty wine glass. "Want more?"

"Noooo. I might get too drunk and let you take advantage of me."

"Is that right?" Marcus chuckled while taking her glass with his and sitting them both on the coffee table beside the couch. "I would never do anything to offend you. Ansinette, I only kissed you in the hallway because I thought you wanted it."

She licked her lips while staring at his. "You did more than kiss me."

"Ansinette, I told you, it's not about . . ."

Ansinette took his chin in her palms and kissed him. She had been waiting for Anthony to fall asleep. They could have crept off to her bedroom while the kids enjoyed the movies, but she couldn't do it that way. Knowing they were in the next room awake wouldn't allow her to lose herself in the moment.

With Anthony and David asleep, she kissed Marcus with silent abandon. He responded with equal passion, scooting closer and fondling her. His groping hands avoided her erogenous zones to grip the flesh above her hip. They both knew where the night was leading, but she needed to take her time.

After kissing for a few minutes, they pulled back. She rested her head against the back of the couch. He did likewise. They stared into each other's eyes.

Ansinette licked her lips. "Thank you for dinner. No one has ever done anything as special. It was really nice."

"No guy has cooked for you or taken you out?"

She smacked her lips. "The nicest place my ex took me was Chili's. We never went out, and he wasn't cooking nothing but oatmeal."

"All of that will change now. I know a guy."

He kissed her then, Ansinette lost herself. Her body temperature climbed twenty degrees in the first few seconds that their lips touched. Her hands went to work, tiptoeing over his chest and belly. Her nipples grew so hard that they hurt and begged to be released.

Ansinette stood and lifted Marcus by the hand.

She pointed to the kids then raised a finger to her lips for him to be silent as she led him to her bedroom. Her heart pounded wildly in her chest. She hadn't slept with a man that she *wanted* to be with in a long time. Too long of a time! Her legs were spaghetti. Her knees, jelly. She didn't know how she made it to the bedroom without support.

Marcus closed the door behind them.

MARCUS STOOD NERVOUSLY before Ansinette. He wanted everything to be perfect. He wondered if his breath smelled okay, or if his armpits were fresh. A million self-conscious thoughts crossed his mind in rapid succession. He forced himself to push them away so that he could focus solely on the woman in his arms.

He pressed his lips to hers. She closed the distance and eased against him. His hands slid below her lower back to cup her behind. She expressed her approval by pressing closer to him. His hand dipped beneath the blooming skirt of her dress. He discovered bare flesh where panties should have been. His fingers found the thong as his hand rubbed her ass from top to bottom.

Ansinette walked backward to the bed. He followed like a lapdog in tow. She sat. Her hands caressed his chest. "Take off your shirt," she commanded.

He hurried to unbutton it. Her fingers were tracing the crevices of his abs before he could get it off. He stood before her panting, anxious, and needing her, but it wouldn't do to rush. He noticed her staring at the bulge in his pants. He wondered if he was big enough to please her. She surprised him by gripping his manhood through the front of his pants. He opened his fly and let them fall away. Ansinette fished her fingers into his boxers and pulled out his solid dick.

"My God," she muttered.

She stroked him with one hand, marveling at the length of it. The fingers of her free hand roamed over the contours of his chest and stomach. Her lips kissed the head of his dick.

"Ansinette, baby. You don't have to do that." She didn't reply. Her hands tugged his boxers over his hips, down to his ankles. "Ansinette," he whispered again. Her moist and hot mouth encircled his dick. His eyes rolled up as she suckled the head, flicking her tongue lightly against the tip. "Ansinette. Damn."

She sucked him deeper. Soon she had worked her hands down his pelvis while his dick was halfway down her throat. He saw stars when he closed his eyes. His toes curled from the sensation. She sucked him like that for a long time, then pulled away and pumped him in her fist. She looked up at him, then went in again.

After a few minutes, Marcus felt pressure building in his balls. He tried to push her back. She swatted his hand away and kept busy. He forcefully pulled away and pushed her down on the bed. He climbed between her legs and lay on top of her. "Baby," he whispered. "If you keep doing that, this night will be over sooner than I want it to be." He kissed her.

She grinded her pussy against his dick, her body calling to him. "Turn on the light," she whispered.

Slowly Marcus stood and strode to the wall. He flipped the switch. Light flooded the room. She stood at the edge of the bed when he turned around. Her eyes roamed over his naked body hungrily. He hurried back, but she held him at bay.

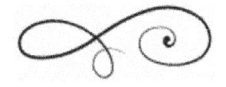

***

ANSINETTE GULPED as she grasped the bottom of her

dress. She had not disrobed in front of a man in a long time. She had only removed her pants and he'd slide her panties to the side when Devon made love to her. The imperfections of her body shamed her, but she wanted to change that about herself. She felt that she had no reason to feel self-conscious around Marcus. It was important for him to see her at her most vulnerable. Perhaps if she bared herself to him, he would open up to her. She lifted the dress over her head.

She watched his eyes drop to her heavy, chocolate-tipped breasts. He gasped at the sight of them. His gaze traveled farther down to the white thong she had worn for him. Only after relishing the hunger in his eyes did she allow him near. She trembled when he took her in his arms. One hand cupped her ass cheek. The other scooped up a fat breast to shove a nipple in his mouth. Her head rolled back in delight: His dick was a missile, wedging between them, trying to force its way into her.

It didn't take long for Marcus' hands to make their way around to her moist middle. He massaged her pussy through the panties, but that wasn't enough. Marcus knelt at her feet and pulled her panties down. Ansinette held onto his shoulders as she stepped out of them. He laid her down on the bed.

Her legs spread wide open. Marcus climbed between them to suck her titties and kiss her neck. His fingers explored her wet spot until she thought she would lose her mind. He began kissing a trail down her belly. She stopped him by tugging his chin back up.

He wore a puzzled expression in his eyes. "I want to taste you."

"Not tonight," she said. "It's late. I want to feel you in me, and then I want to sleep.

We've got all the time in the world."

Marcus didn't argue. He lay on top of her again kissing her lips. Ansinette's hand stole between them to get a firm grip on his dick. It wasn't massive, but it was thick and longer than what she was used to. She hoped it wouldn't hurt her.

MARCUS COULDN'T BELIEVE how tight she was. He didn't get halfway in before she started going crazy on him, bucking to force him deeper. She moaned his name a thousand times. He sunk a little deeper each time that he pushed in. Finally, her body accepted the length of him. Ansinette let out a long gasp when he hit her bottom. Her arms hugged his neck. Her legs circled his waist.

He laid comfortably above her keeping the brunt of his weight on his elbows. She was so thick and lovely. Her skin was the hue of dark chocolate and tasted just as sweet. He slid his dick in and out of her slowly, inching into her body, so that he could savor every second of it.

Ansinette rolled her hips in a circle to encourage him. Soon, she met his movements with thrusts of her own so that their bodies slapped together with tension, whether he wanted it or not. He picked up the pace to please her.

Marcus planted his hands in the crooks behind her knees and fucked her with a steady rhythm. Her hands massaged her own breasts. She pinched her nipples while licking her lips at him. The sight made him want to come right then, but he held back, determined to give her as much pleasure as he could.

Her eyes closed. Her breathing grew shallow and harsh.

Marcus fucked her harder. He pressed her legs so far back that her knees rested beside her head. His dick speared her deeply now, stretching her insides and coming out drenched in her excitement. A low grunt escaped her throat. Then a moan. Her eyes squeezed tight. He knew she was on the verge of an orgasm, and he wanted to push her over the edge. He let go and lay on top of her again. Each time he pushed in, he slammed his pelvis into her clit to maximize her pleasure.

Ansinette's whole body went rigid. She squealed softly as she came, he assumed not to wake her kids. He fucked her hard, until her body relaxed, and he knew he had pleased her. He could have stopped then. It wasn't about his pleasure. But she let him fuck her until he lost his breath and his own desire loomed on the horizon.

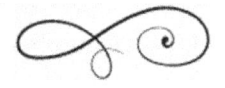

SHE SENSED HIS ORGASM and pushed him away. They weren't wearing a condom, and she didn't want to get pregnant. She flipped him onto his back and lay down beside him with her face in his lap. Ansinette took him in her mouth again, this time jacking him off as she sucked him. Marcus grabbed the back of her head, not to guide her, but to encourage her.

"Baby . . . " he muttered. "Move your mouth. I'm about to . . ."

She jacked him furiously. "I want to see it," she whispered, then sucked him one more time. "Please, let me see it."

   She flicked her tongue over his dick just as he erupted all over her lips and hand. She kept pumping while smiling up at him until he lost his erection and they were both spent.

Ten

ANSINETTE

SHE AWOKE TO BIRDS chirping outside her window, Marcus arm lay draped over her bare belly. She looked over at him. His face rested on the same pillow as her head. She reached out to stroke his shoulder. He stirred, then rolled onto his back.

Ansinette shifted to her side and stared at him. His massive chest heaved with each inhalation. The quiet of the room carried the sound of his heartbeat to her ears. She rested a hand on his chest. Surprisingly, she did not feel awkward about waking up next to him. Marcus belonged in her bed. She knew that now. Had always known it somehow. The hard part proved forcing herself to admit how she felt.

The apartment beyond her closed door seemed a cruel world outside of their paradise. She could stay in her bedroom forever and be fine. Her ears perked. The bells and whistles of a video game wafted faintly to her ears. That was the sound she wanted to hear.

Ansinette nuzzled her lips close to Marcus' neck. Her hand dipped beneath the comforter and found his manhood. It was soft and heavy in her small hand. She massaged his balls gently, just hard enough to get a rise out of him, but not forceful enough to wake him. Her eyes watched him as he slept, spying for any signs of discomfort.

It didn't take long for him to grow erect and fat in her palm. She pulled back the blanket. His dick looked much bigger than she remembered. Masterpieces hanging in art museums couldn't compare to his penis. She thought of sending a picture to Robin, just to make her jealous. She wouldn't really do that, but the thought pleased her.

Ansinette wrapped her fist firmly around Marcus' dick and stroked him. Her pussy yearned to swallow him up, but she made herself wait. Under normal circumstances she would never molest a man in his sleep, but this one took her way out of the realm of normal. Ansinette would marry him if he asked, even though they hadn't known each other for long.

His eyes fluttered suddenly. He moaned a bit. Ansinette's hand stopped pumping, but she kept a firm grip on him. She looked down at his dick. She wanted it inside her so bad. She didn't care if he awoke, but the game of letting him sleep while she took her pleasure excited her. Seconds later his breathing eased. He drifted back into a peaceful slumber. She giggled quietly at her mischief. She stroked him again, this time slower and with less vigor. Her lips kissed a gentle trail down his chest until her mouth closed around his nipple and licked him there. Still he did not wake.

She was sopping wet now with no plans to masturbate.

Ansinette sat up and threw one leg over his waist as softly as she could. He did not move. One of her knees rested on the mattress, the other foot planted beside him, so that she was half kneeling while straddling him. She lifted up enough to guide him into her quivering pussy. Soreness from the night before gave her caution. She hoped the pain would yield to pleasure once she got started. She had plans to abuse her body in many sensual ways.

She eased him into her. Her body tingled at the feel of him in every conceivable centimeter. She settled all the way down, feeling him deep in her belly, but she did not rest all of her weight on him. Moderately, she slid him in and out hoping not to wake him.

"Marcus . . . " she whispered, scooping her pelvis to bury him deep. "Don't wake up, baby. Please don't wake up."

Her hands cupped her breasts. Her nipples stiffened to pebbles as she pinched them. She looked down on Marcus. His eyes remained closed. His mouth a mask of serenity. His dick felt huge in her. She wondered about the dream he was having—if it was about her. She prayed that it was because he was the man of her dreams.

She wanted him deeper, but she didn't want to wake him. Yet, her body was screaming for more. Fuck it. She had to take the risk. What was the worst that could happen? He'd wake up with his dick a foot deep in the best pussy he ever had. What man wouldn't want to wake up to that?

Her standing leg lowered to its knee. She lay all of her weight on him, loving the way her breasts smashed against his chest. Her arms cradled the side of his face. She stared at him as she rode slowly, grinding her clit against his belly. *Don't wake up Marcus*, she thought.

She fucked him unhurriedly like that for what seemed like an eternity. She held her orgasm at bay for as long as she could. Her body yearned to ride him harder, but she kept a snail's pace.

Marcus grunted as his hands grabbed the voluptuous cheeks of her ass.

"Marcus," she whispered, looking into his open eyes.

He lifted her a little and fucked her from the bottom, holding her ass wide open. She lost herself as he took control. Ansinette slammed her pussy into him, impaling herself on his big dick.

"Shit," she murmured. "Give it to me. Give me that dick."

Her pussy gripped him like a tight leather glove as she came, drawing out soft yelps from her. He rammed into her, tearing her insides up.

"Fuck me, Marcus," she panted. "Fuck me with that big dick."

Her drawn out orgasm seemed to last forever. When the last of the convulsions wracked her body, Ansinette lay on him for a moment to catch her breath. She felt electric. She felt drained, but she knew that she could have a million more orgasms and never get enough. She rose up and started riding him again with her hands planted firmly on his chest. This time, she could ride him like she wanted to.

Marcus reached up to squeeze her heavy titties. They were so big that they spilled out of the side of his hands even though he had a full grip. He held them tight, enjoying the way she stared at him. He sat up and suckled one pert nipple, coaxing a sharp gasp from her. Ansinette felt another wave of pleasure approaching. She slammed her fat ass against him, jamming his dick in and out of her so hard that she almost cried out in pain.

She bent down just as her orgasm began, planting kisses against his lips.

"Ansinette, I'm going to let loose, baby. Get up . . . "

"No . . ." she said. "I don't care."

She kept riding him. She fucked his dick until she felt it jerk inside of her and spurt his seed deep into her womb. The orgasm seized her body violently, and she could no longer move. She could only lay still as she milked him dry.

Sometime later, after they had both been satisfied and lay quiet, she rolled off and snuggled in close to him. He covered them with the blanket. They lay staring into each other's eyes.

Marcus grinned. "You're a freak."

A guttural laugh rumbled in her belly. "You were awake the whole time, weren't you?"

"Long before you knew it."

"Just so you know, I have never done anything like that before."

He raised an eyebrow. "I'm special?"

She winked.

Marcus hugged her closer. "Don't holler if I wake you up the same way."

She kissed his lips, morning breath and all, then said. "I can't wait."

His erection was still raging stiff between them. Her hands dipped beneath the covers to stroke him. She threw a leg over his waist and eased in closer determined to make the most of their morning.

Just as she slid him inside for the second time a banging knock on her bedroom door startled them. Ansinette hopped up wild-eyed, thinking of her children and fearing the worst. "What is it?" She shouted.

Through the door, Anthony said, "My dad is outside. He keeps knocking and telling me to open the door. He said he's going to whip me if I don't let him in."

"Just a minute." Ansinette looked over and saw Marcus hurrying to slide on the slacks he wore the night before. "Don't let him in," she called to Anthony. Her robe hung on a corner of the closet door. She grabbed the garment and slung it around her shoulders in one motion. "I'll be out soon."

Anthony responded. "Okay."

She tied the robe and stepped into a pink pair of fuzzy slippers. Marcus buttoned his pants. He stood before her bare chested and waiting for her to tell him what to do. "Stay in here," she whispered to him.

Marcus sneered. "I'm not afraid of him."

"It's not about that, Marcus. Just—just stay here. Please. I'll make him leave."

Marcus frowned, but relented. "Alright." As an afterthought he said, "If he yells at you or does anything crazy..."

Ansinette had the door open already. "Stay here."

Anthony and David stood sheepishly beside the door. They parted when she arrived. Three pounding thumps shook the door on its hinges. She stepped to the door looking like Crackhead Tina with a lopsided afro and sleep eyes. She moved to peek out of the peephole, but the knocks came again, giving her pause. Ansinette turned to Anthony and David. "Go to your room!" They took off running.

She waited a moment, then pressed her eye to the peephole. Devon paced outside of her apartment. His receding hairline made his forehead bulge ten times bigger in the fisheye lens of the spyglass. He resembled George Jefferson with good hair.

"Why are you banging on my door, Devon?"

"Open up, Ansinette. I've been texting and calling you for three days. This is the only way I could get your attention. I need to talk to you."

She had to admit that he sounded serious. "Are you going to act like you have some sense?"

"Open the damned door."

"Do you have a mask?"

"Yes, Ansinette. It's in my pocket."

"A lot of good it's going to do in there. Put it on. I won't risk my kids' lives because you're pissed off."

"Goddamn it." Devon reached into his pocket to pull out the black facemask. He slipped it on. "Happy now?"

"Six feet, Devon. Social distancing."

He backed up to the far wall of the breezeway.

Ansinette kept the chain on the door when she opened it. "What's so important that you had to wake us up all hours of the morning?"

Devon stood at the door like he wanted to kick it in. "Ansinette, I didn't come out here to play with you. Open the door, please."

"It's open enough. What do you want?"

"To see my kids."

Ansinette sucked her teeth. "You never wanted to see them before."

Devon stood on his tiptoes in an attempt to peer into the apartment. "Who is that?" Ansinette pushed the door closed and looked behind her toward the back hall. No one stood there. She cursed silently, knowing that Devon had tricked her. He stood with a satisfied smirk when she opened the door again.

He asked, "Who did you think I saw in there? Marcus Jenkins?"

The sound of Marcus' full name left her nearly speechless. "What?"

"Marcus Jenkins. Used to live right . . . " He pointed to Marcus' vacant apartment. "There." Devon waited for Ansinette to speak, when she didn't, he said, "That's who it is, isn't it?"

"I don't know what you're talking about. No one is here."

Devon shook his head. "When I heard his name the other day. I figured that's who it was. Wasn't too hard to find out his full name. All I had to do was search his apartment's address. After that, I learned all I could have ever hoped to know."

"What's the point, Devon?"

"You've got a rapist living in the same house as my sons."

"He's not . . . "

"He is! Don't lie to me. I'll file a paternity suit so fast that it'll straighten that nappy-ass natural hair on your head. I'm a public servant, Ansinette. I know people. Police chiefs. Lawyers. There isn't a judge this side of North Carolina that wouldn't vouch for my character and give me full custody if I asked for it. Act stupid if you want to."

If she hadn't been holding onto the doorknob, she would have crumpled to the floor. "There's—there's nobody here, Devon. Just me and the boys."

"Let me see for myself. Open the door."

"This is my house, Devon. I don't have to let you in, and I find it funny that you can sleep with who you want, but as soon as you think I have somebody, you threaten to take my kids from me. What kind of man are you?"

"I'm not playing with you, Ansinette."

"If that's all you came over here for, we don't have anything else to talk about. I'll let you see the boys when it's safe. You're not coming in here right now. Not when I don't know what strange woman is sharing your bed. There's no telling what diseases you're carrying."

Devon shrugged. "Okay. Since you want to play like that, I'll leave. But don't expect a check from me this month. Don't expect a dime anytime soon."

Ansinette's heart sank. "Devon, you know that we need that money. Don't take your anger out on the boys. They haven't done anything wrong to you. All they want is a father, and you won't even be that."

He started down the stairs. "It is what it is. If I find out that Marcus is living with you, I'll take the boys. I promise you that."

Eleven

MARCUS

MARCUS RAN TO ANSINETTE as soon as she closed the front door. She faced him—her expression a mask of exhaustion—and leaned against the wall. He had not expected her to look so distraught. "What did he want?" Marcus asked her.

She opened her mouth to speak. Nothing came out. She lowered her eyes to focus on the floor. "Marcus . . ."

Marcus reached out to grasp her shoulder. She shrank away. "Ansinette. Baby, what's wrong?"

Her tears spoke the words her mouth would not. Marcus watched silently as she hugged herself and hurried to her bedroom. The door slammed shortly after.

Anthony and David crept out of their bedroom seconds later. Both found it difficult to meet Marcus' eyes. "What's wrong with my mom?" Anthony asked him.

Marcus leaned against the wall. "I don't know."

None of them spoke after that. Anthony and David were too young to understand adult drama, but they were old enough to know it wasn't their business. Anthony nudged David back into the bedroom. He looked at Marcus one last time before disappearing in there himself.

Marcus made his way to Ansinette's door. His fist moved to knock, but he thought better of it. Her muffled sobs could be heard. He didn't stay long.

Inside his room, Marcus sat on the floor beside his sleeping bag. He checked his phone. Three texts. His mom texted twice. Tony left a link and a message reading: *check this out*. Marcus clicked the link. It led to a video of federal legislators passing a Coronavirus stimulus package. Every household was set to receive at least twelve hundred dollars. Under normal circumstances, he would have been ecstatic, but even the prospect of free money didn't excite him.

His mother called as he was putting his phone down. "How are you, Mom?"

"Bored out of my damn mind," she said. "Can't leave the house. I've cleaned up. Fixed everything that was broken. Now I'm tired and irritable. How is everything at your girlfriend's house?"

He allowed her jab to go unchecked. "I don't know. We like each other, Mama. But her ex came over this morning." He explained what he knew, all the way up to the point where she had locked herself in her bedroom.

Betty listened quietly. When Marcus finished, she said, "You don't know what kind of history her and that man have. Children bind a couple for life, in ways that you may never understand because you don't have kids."

"They aren't together," he complained. "Why should he

have control of her?"

"Marcus, you will never be able to break that bond. If you care about her, the first thing you need to do is accept that. Support her."

He listened and he understood that his mother knew more about such situations than he did. "What should I do, Mama? She won't talk to me."

"Give her time. She won't stay locked in there forever. She has to eat. But whatever you do, don't rush. Let her figure out what she's feeling. She'll come to you when she's ready."

Marcus promised to heed her advice before hanging up. After talking to his mom, he checked his emails. Nothing by spam. He'd heard nothing from Panda, the tech company he had recently interviewed with. If there were ever a time to start a new job, it was now. He dropped his phone and stared at the floor.

Thoughts of Ansinette saddened him. Maybe he'd rushed into things. Maybe they shouldn't have made love. Sex always fucked things up, no matter who he had sex with. It had a way of complicating things to catastrophic proportions. Marcus had no idea what he had done for Ansinette to shut him out.

Moving into her apartment for a few weeks once seemed like a good idea. Not anymore. He may have been better off sleeping in his truck. He would've been cramped, but at least he wouldn't feel half as bad as he did. He kept thinking that Devon confronted Ansinette about him somehow. He wasn't sure. Then again, maybe it didn't have anything to do with him. His mom might have been right. Ansinette needed time to think.

He decided to give her that time.

Marcus picked up his phone and speed dialed Tony. They connected on the third ring. "Tony," Marcus said. "do you still have that open couch in your man cave?"

Thirty minutes later, he had showered and packed his belongings. Packing didn't take long because he had one suitcase.

Ansinette leaned in his doorway wearing gray cotton shorts and a T-shirt as he was rolling up his sleeping bag. She glanced at his full suitcase. "Where are you going?"

Marcus stood up. "I get the feeling that I wore out my welcome. My being here has complicated things. I want you to be happy." He stared at her. Her eyes fell to the floor. "Ansinette, I don't know what else to do."

She looked up then. In her gaze, Marcus saw years of hurt and unfulfilled desire that he did not cause. He saw a woman who wanted to be loved but who didn't know how to accept love. She needed a strong man in her life. A lot of questions came with that realization. Did she know that she needed him? Was she afraid of change? Only she could answer those questions, but he was afraid to ask.

Instead of responding to him, Ansinette turned and hurried back to her bedroom.

"Ansinette."

Marcus stepped out into the hallway. Her bedroom door stood wide open. She sat on the edge of her bed waiting for him.

"Ansinette…"

"Close the door, Marcus."

He did as told, then he rushed to say, "I don't know what I did wrong, but whatever it was, I'm sorry."

A pained expression creased her brows. "You didn't do

anything, Marcus. It's your past. Devon knows that you were in prison. He's threatened to take my boys if he finds out that you're living here."

Hearing the truth sucked the wind out of him. Marcus didn't have a response. He thought he had conquered his past. He overcame every hurdle that stood in his way on the road to becoming a new man. He had a decent job, he had found a place to live with no co-signer, he bought a new truck, and he had money in the bank. Marcus thought those accomplishments would push his past far behind him—so far behind that he wouldn't have to worry about it resurfacing. He was wrong.

Marcus took a step toward her. "Ansinette, it's not what you think. I spent five years in there for nothing. I swear to you."

"Rape, Marcus?" She spat.

He thought of a million explanations. Would any one of them combat whatever bullshit may have been reported on the internet? "You looked me up?"

Ansinette stood. "No, but I know enough. Just thinking that you raped somebody bothers me, Marcus."

"I didn't do that. I would never…"

Ansinette thrust out a flat palm to stop him. She held his gaze for a long time, then walked over to the window with her back turned to him. "You want to know the truth? It doesn't matter to me. I believe you. That's why I didn't read about it."

Marcus stepped behind her but hovered a foot away.

Still, she would not look at him. "I have never met a man like you. I knew it the first time we met. You're kind. Sweet. Thoughtful. And that's what scared me about you. A girl gets used to being abused. Anything short of that raises alarm signals. Men like you are too good to be true. I feel like I know your heart. I don't think you could have done what you went to prison for, but how I feel won't stop Devon from taking Anthony and David."

He stepped closer until his belly brushed her back and his lips nuzzled her ear as he asked, "Do you want me to leave?"

She leaned into him. "No. I want you to love me."

His arms circled her waist. He kissed her neck and held her close.

Outside, he saw a group of kids in the parking lot kicking a soccer ball. They stood at least ten feet apart. They all wore masks and would not touch the ball with their hands, only their feet. The way they played was a display of the state of the world. People wanted to be close. Intimacy was an integral part of human existence. But the threat of disease and hurt kept them apart. The same could be said of his and Ansinette's relationship. Their pasts threatened to draw a wedge between them, and he was determined not to let that happen.

Marcus kissed her ear. "We'll fight him in the courts."

"I don't see a way around it. He'll stop giving me money until the courts force him to pay child support. I'm working, but I don't make enough to support three hungry mouths. Not comfortably."

"They've been talking about a Coronavirus stimulus. Twelve-hundred dollars."

"Okay," she said. "When that's gone, then what?"

He smiled some. "I'm gainfully employed."

Ansinette giggled. "You gonna move in?"

He hugged her closer. "I already have."

She turned her mouth to the side and kissed him. Her tongue tasted of honey and vanilla. "The boys love you."

"Just the boys?"

"For now. Give me some time. You'll grow on me."

"Like a fungus." He kissed her again, loving the feel of her ass pressed against his crotch.

As Marcus held her, he couldn't help but feel confident that they would be okay. He didn't care what Devon did. He could never disrupt the way they felt about each other. He made up his mind right then to have Ansinette's back, no matter what.

They stood there kissing for a long time with the sun beaming on them through the open window. The children put away their ball and went home for the day. The parking lot stood empty and silent. His hands pinched her soft belly, then moved up to her pendulous breasts. He pulled up her bra and squeezed warm nipples. Ansinette moaned and pressed her ass harder into his growing erection.

She guided one of his hands inside the front of her shorts. She wore no panties. Marcus found her clit above her slippery opening and fondled it. Ansinette reached behind her to grab his dick through his pants. He wanted her to suck him again, but he owed her a favor.

Gently, Marcus slid Ansinette's shorts down over her hips and knelt to help her step out or them. She tried to face him, but he pushed her back so that her hands were forced to grip the windowsill. "Somebody might see us," she whispered.

"They won't see this," he stated.

He spread her legs wide as he knelt on his knees behind her. His hand pried her ass apart, and he dipped his head low and licked her pussy from behind. Ansinette got the idea and bent over farther, giving him complete access to her hot and wet opening. Marcus lapped at it like a thirsty dog at a water fountain.

Ansinette's hips rolled in a circle. "Your tongue is so hot . . ."

Her hands gripped her own ass cheeks and held them open. Marcus dipped lower and pulled her pussy apart. His tongue took long licks from the front to the back. He found her clit and sucked it into his mouth. Ansinette squealed as he ate her. Marcus kept it up, licking faster and faster, teasing her clit until she cried out in ecstasy. He burrowed his face deep in her ass and plunged his tongue inside her pussy, licking her walls until she came in his mouth.

He stood quickly when she was done. His fingers hurried to open his pants. Ansinette reached behind her to fondle his dick while he tried to free it. "Hurry up," she murmured. "I want it bad. Hurry. Marcus. Hurry."

His dick strained against his clothes. He kept looking down at the soft cheeks of her fat ass and yearned to be inside of it. His hands gripped her hips and pumped into her before he got his pants all the way down. He let out a gasp as he hit her bottom, loving how her hot pussy felt around his dick. He fucked her slowly at first. She moved against him, throwing it back. He felt her hands cup his balls beneath them. He almost lost it then, but he held on, wanting to enjoy every second of their union.

Ansinette stood and pressed her back into his chest. Marcus' finger sunk low and fondled her clit as he fucked her.

"Deeper," she whispered.

Marcus took long strokes and slid back in as far as he could go.

"Deeper," she whispered again.

He pulled back and pushed in forcefully this time, feeling his dick bump her limit.

"Deeper, baby. Harder. Fuck me harder, Marcus. Give me that big dick. I love that dick. Fuck me. Hurt me."

His hands clawed at her titties now. He pulled out so far that his dick slipped out with each thrust and rammed back in. He fucked her so deeply that he stretched her out, yet she begged him to punish her more.

"That's it, Marcus," she cried out. "Make me come."

He sucked wind at a ragged pace as he fucked the shit out of her. Hearing her cries brought his pleasure to its boiling point. Her pussy became wetter as she came, running down his legs. He pulled out just as he was exploding and shot out all over her juicy ass cheeks.

She turned and kissed him, then whispered, "You're going to make it hard for me not to fall in love."

Twelve

ANSINETTE

ROBIN PICKED UP on the first ring. Ansinette spotted her queen-sized bed in the background of the FaceTime. Robin wore a white silk robe and had her natural hair tied with a scarf that cascaded down the front of her shoulder.

"You look sober," Ansinette remarked.

Robin beamed and whispered, "I am!"

Ansinette squinted at her sister. "Why are you whispering?"

Robin bit her bottom lip, then swiveled her phone so that Ansinette could see the sleeping figure in her bed.

Ansinette squealed. "Who is that?"

Robin pressed a hand to her mouth to stifle her giggle as she hurried out of the bedroom. She entered the bathroom and eased the door closed behind her. To Ansinette she said, "There is no D like new D."

THE VIRUS BROUGHT ME MY FIRST LOVE

Ansinette sat on the edge of her bed stunned. "Where did you find a man during the pandemic?"

Robin looked mildly offended. "What, you think you're the only one?" Robin sniffed the air. "You smell like sex yourself."

"We're not talking about me, Robin."

Robin rolled her eyes. "I am so bad. I know it. I'm terrible."

"What did you do?"

"I ordered a pizza. Extra sausage. You know what I like. Well, the delivery guy showed up, and girl, he looked so good in his little Dominoes shirt and skinny jeans."

Ansinette imagined the scene. Robin stood half-dressed in that silk robe while standing in her doorway, flustered as she ogled the young delivery man. She asked Robin, "Aren't they supposed to drop the pizza off on the doorstep or something?"

"I asked him to come closer," Robin confessed. "I told him that I had a tip . . . in my house."

"Robin, did you even know his name?"

Robin looked away in shame. She snorted a laugh. "I still don't know it."

"Are you serious? You've got some strange man sleeping in your bed? Probably got him fired. I know he didn't show up back at work. And you don't know his name? What kind of shit are you into?"

"I am so weak. You don't have to remind me."

"How do you know he didn't have the virus?"

"He didn't seem sick to me," Robin whined.

"He could be Asymptomatic. They're carriers, even though they don't show signs."

"It doesn't matter," Robin assured her. "We wore our masks."

"You had sex while wearing your masks?"

Robin patted her hair. "Don't knock it until you try it, honey. I see why women loved *Fifty Shades of Grey*. That freaky-type shit turned me on. I ordered all three books this morning."

Ansinette shook her head. "You could be sick right now."

"I'll be sick if he doesn't give me that dick again before he leaves. I can deal with the Coronavirus for a little while longer. I can't take the loneliness I felt before last night. My God. I didn't realize that I had no life before all of this shit. I was so busy running here and there. I never had time to sit down and really think about how empty I felt inside, how lonely I really was."

Ansinette couldn't fault Robin for how she felt. She had felt the same way. Having Marcus in the house reminded her of how lonely she had been before the lockdown. It was the plight of the single woman. Before the pandemic, her life consisted of work, kids, bills, and work. She had no time to fall in love or to even try. She barely had time to wash her ass in the morning. Let alone worry about smelling good for some man. Being stuck in the house showed her just how boring her life had been.

Robin asked, "You're not mad at me, are you?"

"No. A little worried. You have to be more careful. There's a lot more out there than the Coronavirus."

"I know. But your big sister can take care of herself. Ain't nothing like coffee and dick in the morning. I woke him up a little while ago and put his ass right back to sleep."

Ansinette couldn't help but laugh at that. "I know what

you mean."

Robin raised a quizzical eyebrow. "Let me find out you and Mr. Marcus have been ducking and hiding from your kids."

"Is it that obvious?"

"You weren't lying to anybody but yourself. l knew you were going to fuck him when you let him move in. How many days did that sleeping bag last?"

"About four days."

"That's what I thought. Aw, don't look so sad, Ansinette. If you're enjoying yourself, enjoy it. Life is too short to be lonely. The Coronavirus taught me that the hard way. You like him. Your boys like him. What's the problem?"

Ansinette recounted the drama with Devon the morning before. Robin listened intently, only offering a smack of her lips occasionally when Ansinette expressed her grief.

"He threatened to take your kids?" Robin asked. When Ansinette nodded, Robin shook her head. "That tender-dick ass nigga. He's just mad because you have a real man, and now he knows there will never be anything else between you. He can't raise two boys on his own. Come on now."

"Tell me about it." Ansinette heard the front door of the apartment close. She went to the window and saw Marcus climb in his truck. Just seeing him made her heart flutter. She missed him already, and he hadn't left the parking lot. She looked back to Robin on her phone and sighed. "He doesn't really want custody of Anthony and David. He wants to use them to control me."

Robin thought about that. "What does Marcus say?"

"He wants to beat him up."

"You should let him. He needs a good, size-twelve foot

deep in his soft ass. I would drive to his house and do it myself if I didn't have a slab of beefcake marinating in my satin sheets. It needs constant attention."

Ansinette let off a gut wrenching laugh so raucous that she had to cover her mouth so she wouldn't alert her sons.

Robin went on. "Somebody ought to kick his ass with a pair of spiked stilettos. See how he likes that."

"You're crazy."

"Am I lying?"

Ansinette bit the inside of her cheek to stifle her laugh. "I can't believe I'm entertaining this."

"What? Ansinette? After all that little-dick motherfucker has done to you?"

"You're right." Ansinette admitted. "He does need his ass kicked. I don't understand why he can't accept that I don't want to be with him. Love your children and leave me the hell alone."

"Do you think he would react the same way if Marcus hadn't been to prison?"

Ansinette had thought about it. "I don't know." She realized that it didn't matter who laid in her bed. Devon would be jealous regardless. It was a pride thing. "He's using Marcus' background as an excuse to complain."

Robin's amused expression dissipated. "Has Marcus told you about his crime yet?"

"Why do you have to call it his crime? It doesn't define him. And no, we haven't discussed it."

"Don't you want to know?"

"Robin, whatever happened, happened in the past. He says he didn't do it. I have no reason not to believe him."

"Ansinette. Serious talk now. Don't you want to know?

When I'm with a guy, I want to know everything about him. Leave no stone unturned."

"This from a bitch who doesn't even know the negro's name who is laid up in her bed as we speak. You're a piece of work, you know that? All up in mine."

"Hold up, hold up!" Robin interrupted. "I said a man that *I am with*. Me and–what's his face–are fucking. There's a difference. I tripped and fell on a dick. You're playing house and shit."

"Robin, stay out of my business. He'll tell me when he's good and ready. Until then, I'm fine with not knowing. I won't hold him accountable for something he did or didn't do years ago. When you love somebody, none of that matters. You have to look past all of that."

Robin sat silent and stared off into space. After some time, she asked, "You love him?"

Ansinette ran a shaky hand over her forehead. It was hard to meet her sister's eyes. "Love is a complicated word. I think I could. And I don't want to mess it up. Whatever happened in his past hurt him deeply. He's living with scars that I can't help him heal. If I was going through that, I would talk about it when I was ready. Not a moment sooner. He's getting his life together, and I'm determined to help him."

"I won't bring it up anymore. I thought I was helping."

"Support me," Ansinette said. "That's how you can help."

"I've got your back. You know that. Where's he at now?"

"He went to the store."

Robin offered a sly smile. "At least he's got his own money. A lot of black men don't have a job and aren't trying to look for one. They have their hand out every time they meet a woman with a little piece of a job."

"He's been doing great. He's a college graduate. And he's looking for a better job. That's the point I'm trying to make. Too many women look for reasons to tear a man down. I want to help build him up."

"You'd better stay on him to keep him straight. A nigga can say what he wants. I need to see some action. You'll be paying all the bills before you know it."

Ansinette had already thought about the consequences of living with a man who had been laid off. In the beginning, he was only supposed to stay for a few weeks. Now, Ansinette didn't want him to ever leave. Of all the drama with Devon, Marcus finding a job seemed like a small thing. They will make it. They can make it work.

Ansinette told Robin, "There's more to life than money."

"Like what? A dick doesn't stay hard forever. And don't forget that you have to feed that motherfucker too."

"We'll be fine," Ansinette assured Robin. "Life won't always be bad. I'm due for a much deserved happy ending."

"I feel you but remember what Mama used to say: It'll get worse before it gets better."

Thirteen

MARCUS

DAVID WAS SITTING ON THE COUCH watching ESPN when Marcus made it home from the store. The boy tossed his football into the air and caught it absentmindedly. Marcus watched him for a moment before carrying a bundle of toilet paper to the back. He stripped and showered. Next, he tossed the clothes that he'd worn to the store in the washing machine. Ansinette sat at the computer in her bedroom when he checked in on her.

Marcus kissed her cheek. "Did you miss me as much as I missed you?"

"Not now, Marcus. I needed to have this contract written yesterday. I've got a meeting on Zoom in thirty minutes and I am not prepared."

He backed up to give her some space. Despite her brevity, he admired her work ethic. She knew how to get a job done. "Okay, I'll see you in a little bit."

Ansinette smiled at him as he walked to the door. "You're going to see a lot of me later. Maybe more than you can handle." She bit her bottom lip. Marcus smiled and headed out of the room. "Marcus," she called out. "Give me some more sugar before you go." He walked back and leaned down to kiss her. She held it for much longer than she should have, but he didn't mind at all. When she pulled back, she said, "You're worse than a narcotic. I can't get enough of you."

He walked to the door. "Finish your work. I'll give you a fix when you're done."

Marcus closed the door behind him when he walked out. Next, he opened the boys' bedroom door. Anthony lay sprawled out on the floor napping. Instead of a video game controller in his hand, he loosely held a pencil. His history book lay open beside him, and it looked as if he was on the road to finishing his assignment.

Marcus pulled the door closed and stood there in thought. Life presented more surprises than he was prepared for. Not too long ago he was a bachelor. Now he had a family. If someone had told him that he'd be at this point in his life a month ago, he would have called them crazy. His past fears of fatherhood fell to the wayside as he began to think that he would make a great stepdad. Maybe he could be the father he never had and always wanted. He hoped that he could. Not only did Anthony and David need a man in their lives, Marcus needed them to make him feel complete.

He strode into the living room where David was still

watching ESPN. Stephen A. Smith argued with Max Kellerman about the Dallas Cowboys football team stalling on renewing a contract with the quarterback, Dak Prescott. David tossed his football in the air and caught it. He kept his eyes focused on the TV, soaking up every word.

Marcus headed to the kitchen for a drink. "David. You hungry?"

"Ate some cereal."

"A drink?"

David still did not look away from the television. "Kool-Aid."

Marcus poured two glasses with ice and headed back to the living room. He plopped down on the couch next to David. The boy guzzled half the glass as soon as it touched his hand. His eyes remained glued to the broadcast the entire time.

David muttered, "Thanks," without looking at Marcus.

On TV, footage of Dak Prescott stretching filled the screen. Marcus noticed how David perked up when the station switched to game footage. Dak faked a handoff to the running back, Ezekiel Elliott, then threw a deep ball straight to the end zone for a touchdown.

Marcus looked at David. "You a Cowboys' fan?"

"Raiders."

Marcus chuckled. "They haven't won anything since before I was born."

"They'll do better in Las Vegas. Besides, I like their uniforms." David admitted. "Pirates."

"I won't argue with that." He watched the sports commentary a little longer. Jerry Jones, owner of the Cowboys, used Zoom to join the broadcast swearing that he planned to pay Dak all that he was worth. When another shot of Dak running hard for a touchdown crossed the screen, Marcus told David. "A lot of people don't think Dak is worth a big contract. What do you think?"

"I don't understand why. He's a beast. He hasn't produced in big games, but maybe that's because he doesn't have the experience."

"Neither does Patrick Mahomes, but he won a Superbowl."

David shrugged. "With Dak and Ezekiel Elliott, they should have been in the Superbowl by now. Maybe the new coaching staff will get them up to speed. Jason Garret was a has been anyway."

Marcus almost forgot that he was talking to a kid. "Been watching ESPN long?"

"My entire life," David commented seriously.

"Nine whole years, huh?"

"It's almost a decade."

"Almost." Marcus stared at David. "Why don't you play football? You know enough about it."

David shrugged. "Mom won't let me. She said I could get brain damage. I keep telling her that if I make it to the NFL, I won't need my brain. All I'll have to be able to do is count money."

Marcus rubbed his head. "It's not that easy, champ. Football players are some of the most intelligent men you will ever meet. Playing football doesn't only consist of grabbing the ball and running to the end zone. It's a game of strategy. I had a high school coach that used to make us play chess before every game. He'd have twelve boards set up on card tables when we came into the locker room. He said that he wanted us to think about every move we made on the field in the same way that we thought about every move in a game of chess."

David looked to him. "Were y'all any good?"

Marcus nodded nonchalantly. "Two state championships. My junior and senior year." "Chess helped you win at football?"

"Think about it, we had thirty or forty plays to memorize. It wasn't enough for each player to know what he had to do on the field. He had to know where every player was going to be at all times. A team is a single unit that has to work together in order to win. Chess is no different. A good chess player learns how the pieces move together. Chess. Football. War. They all share strategies."

"I'll bet you were the smartest guy on your team."

"Nah. The quarterback ran the show. He had to read the defense and know where to put the ball. Me? I was the fastest. I learned my position and worked hard to be the best at it."

David turned to get a better look at Marcus. "What position did you play? Wide receiver?"

"Running back."

David's eyes lit up. "Like Ezekiel Elliot? Were you that fast?"

"Let's see." Marcus pulled his phone from his pocket and googled his name. A link to a news story reporting on his incarceration stood at the top of the list. He paused, then swiped until he found a link that he wanted. "This was when we played in the Sugar Bowl against Florida State University. I started my freshman year."

David leaned over to stare at the phone.

"Hold on," Marcus said. He linked his phone to the TV. An image of him as a nineteen-year-old kid filled the screen.

"You started for Louisiana State University?"

Marcus smiled at David's excitement. No one had ever reacted so enthusiastically about his football days. He played the video. "We lost," Marcus said. "But that was the best game I played in my life."

"Did you put up big numbers?"

Footage of LSU at FSU's twenty-yard line crossed the screen. Marcus hunched in the backfield. The quarterback snapped the ball and handed it off to Marcus who shifted ten yards toward a gap in the line of scrimmage. He blasted through the hole and had a clear shot straight up the field. Once he burst through, no one could catch him. He dropped the ball in the end zone as his team swarmed him with congratulations.

David sat speechless.

The footage continued. Marcus draped his arm over the back of the couch. He hadn't watched any of his old football games in years. His past success stabbed him with regret each time he stepped backward into that time. A wave of depression swept over him and threatened to carry him away. David's smile helped to ease his tension. Play after play, David whooped and hollered when Marcus scored a touchdown. Marcus' masterful performance was only overshadowed by the juggernaut that was FSU, steamrolling over the LSU defense to achieve a 53-37 victory.

When that game was over, David begged him to play more. The boy insisted that Marcus rewind the footage and breakdown the plays. The joy of Marcus' day didn't come from reveling in his past triumphs. He gained happiness from teaching little David something about life that he couldn't learn from anyone else.

Not long after they started watching the footage, Anthony stepped into the living room rubbing sleep from his eyes. He sat down to watch the games with them, amazed that a celebrity was living in his house.

"Why didn't you tell us before?" Anthony asked.

"I played football in college. It was no big deal."

David stood up excitedly. "Why didn't you play in the NFL? You could have been rich."

Marcus felt a twinge of pain in his heart. "I wasn't that good."

"Looked like it to me," Anthony butted in.

"Yeah," David added. "What happened?"

Marcus sank into the couch and stared at his still image on the TV screen. He looked larger than life, like a modern-day gladiator in his football uniform, like a warrior prepared for battle. He loved every minute of it when he played. The traveling. The attention. The women. He didn't make a dime while he played college ball, but the experience seemed worth its weight in gold.

What did happen?

ANSINETTE

ANSINETTE NEVER THOUGHT SHE would meet a man that could make her feel so good. It seemed like she had an orgasm every time his skin brushed against hers. She had been with other men–men who proved to be boys when compared with this one. His lips were fire against her cool neck as he kissed her there, making her cringe from the sensation. His fondling hands pinched and pulled her tender flesh, kneading tight places that needed loosening. She gasped in delight and felt like screaming her joy. If her sons weren't in the other room playing video games, she would cry out declaring her satisfaction to all who cared to hear. But her sons were in the other room. There were some moments a mother was supposed to enjoy alone. She didn't want any rug-rats to spoil it. The boys had their time with her. Now it was her time for fun.

They lay beside each other, sprawled out on her bed. Her cotton pajamas bunched in all the wrong crevices, making her wish to rip them off. He wore a tank top and sweats that did nothing to prevent his excitement from jabbing her belly. Her natural hair was nappy and wrapped in the pink scarf she'd been wearing to bed since she was in college. She hadn't made up her face in days. Hadn't left the house in weeks. Not even for a walk. They'd woken up, ate breakfast, and did nothing for the rest of the morning. They hadn't showered yet, but it was okay. The lockdown exposed all secrets. There wasn't much she didn't know about him now. He was the man she wanted to be with. She was sure of it. Quarantining with someone was as close to marriage as two people could get.

Her eyes crept open. The noon sun perched high in a pale blue sky, spread golden stripes of light across the far wall of the open window. She stared out and did not spot a single cloud. The day's beauty reminded her of the beautiful way she felt while wrapped in his arms. He had a way of making her feel beautiful when she looked her worse. No man had ever made her so comfortable–so sure of herself.

He got up and stood at the foot of the bed. Ansinette stared as he pulled off his wife beater tank top. Breath caught in her throat; her eyes graced his tight chest and broad shoulders. His stomach rippled with bulging abs. She unbuttoned her pajama top but left the garment closed a bit to keep her decent. The COVID-19 weight she gained pooled around her belly and behind. She felt comfortable around him, but not that comfortable. He slipped his thumbs into the waistband of his sweatpants and slid them down. He wore no underwear. The sledgehammer she saw between his legs made her bottom lip quiver. Thinking of that long, hard black thing sliding in her made her forget her inhibitions.

"Marcus," she murmured.

He reached out and grabbed her pajama bottoms by the waist. Two strong yanks and they were floating high in the air toward the bedroom door. She wore pink granny panties beneath, and if he cared, he didn't show it. His huge hands spread her brown thighs wide as he climbed on the bed between them, where he laid all of his weight on top of her.

Ansinette's arms were wrapping around the back of Marcus' neck and pulling him down before she realized what she was doing. He responded with another kiss, this one planted softly on her lips. Their tongues mingled in the open space. Her eyes shut tight. Her pajama top slipped open, exposing her dark nipples to his hard chest. Their hearts beat in syncopation like horse hooves running wild toward the passion they both needed and wanted. Her hands roamed the expanse of his cobra-shaped back. Ansinette marveled at his muscles rippling beneath milk chocolate skin as he held her close. Her teeth sank into his shoulder to sample a taste.

"We can wait," he whispered. "If you want to. The boys are in the next room. Tonight is not too far away. They'll be asleep then."

Ansinette silenced him with a kiss. Her hand guided his beneath her panties to the flaming hot spot between her legs and let him feel how ready she was. His finger plunged inside as easily as a dolphin diving in a swimming pool. Ansinette kept her hand between them and gripped his manhood. It was so thick that her fingers barely stretched around it. She stroked him from the base to the tip. Her tongue snaked out and licked a circle around his earlobe. She moaned. He grunted. There would be no waiting today.

Before he entered her, Ansinette smiled up at the ceiling. She couldn't help it. A million thoughts ran through her mind, and she couldn't focus on a single one. She tried in vain to pinpoint when she had fallen for him, but that moment was lost to her. So much had happened in so little time. It was as if she had read her story in a fairytale rather than lived it. He was perfect in each and every way. She couldn't believe they had been perfect strangers just two weeks ago.

The coronavirus pandemic had changed the course of their lives in many more ways than one. Lockdowns, riots, protests . . . thoughts of the last fourteen days whizzed by like a blur as Marcus kissed her again. She closed her eyes.

For one precious second, all she thought of was the feeling of his lips against hers. When he pulled back, images of her working from a computer at home, homeschooling her kids, and losing her sanity while being stuck at home invaded her mind. Marcus' lips closed over a pert nipple. Her pains disappeared once again. They faded so far away that Ansinette closed her eyes tighter to keep them away. She was thankful that Marcus had been on lockdown with her. She could think of no other man she would have liked to spend that maddening and unpredictable time with.

Her hand pressed the tip of his manhood to her slick opening. She gasped as he slipped inside, inch by inch until he filled her up. Her legs draped behind his back as he sank his weight on top of her and settled in. He kissed her once again. His lips telling her how much he appreciated her love in ways that his mouth could never express.

Ansinette didn't want to think about all of the people who had died from the coronavirus or the people who lost their homes, their jobs, and their sanity. She didn't want to think about them, but she couldn't help it. They hated being locked down. Being quarantined had ruined their lives. It had not ruined Ansinette's.

Her arms pulled Marcus closer as he began pumping into her. As they made love, she couldn't help but think about the fateful day their lives changed forever.

MARCUS

MARCUS' MEMORIES OF RUNNING plays on the

football field metamorphosed to him sitting in a jail cell. He stared through a Plexiglas window at officers stuffing his street clothes into a trash bag. The ill-fitting orange jumpsuit itched in places he didn't care to scratch in a holding cell filled with forty or fifty other men.

The first judge told him that he was charged with rape, assault with intent to kill, and kidnapping. Marcus dropped to his knees in a sobbing heap right there in the courtroom. He shouted up to the judge that he was no criminal. It was all a mistake. He was hauled back to jail with no bond, forced to rot in a cell, guilty until proven innocent.

Almost nine months later, his public defender brought him a plea offer for thirty years in prison. There was no way he would cop out to a crime he didn't commit. No way. He went back to his jail cell and begged God to help the authorities discover the truth and to let him go.

An all-white jury found him guilty of all counts a year later. By then, he'd lost weight. The jail food had him weak and unhealthy. He hadn't seen the sun in almost two years. After that all he had to look forward to was endless years of brown prison pants, working as a janitor for less than three dollars a week, and fighting the gangs to keep what little he worked so hard to earn.

Looking at his young self on the TV in Ansinette's living room brought more than memories of playing football to mind. He didn't remember that young man. He was so different now. Those youthful days were a lifetime ago. Looking at that kid on TV was like looking at a stranger.

"What happened?" Anthony asked him. "Why didn't you go to the NFL?"

Marcus stood and gestured for David to throw him the

ball. "I guess God had another plan." Marcus beckoned the boys to him. He put the ball in Anthony's hands. "Ant, you're the QB. Dave, you're the running back." He faced them and spread his arms wide. "This is the defensive line. When Ant calls the snap, Dave, you jook to your left, then run right. Ant will hand you the ball. There's a hole in the line of scrimmage right here. Once you get through, you've got a clear shot to the end zone. Got it?"

Both boys nodded and hunched in their positions.

Marcus knelt in front of them.

Anthony called out, "Green twenty-seven! Green twenty-seven!"

Marcus looked up and caught Ansinette leaning against the far wall watching them. Her arms were crossed over her chest, but she wore a proud smile. She gestured for them to continue.

Anthony hollered, "Hut!"

Fourteen

ANSINETTE

ANSINETTE'S MEETING RAN LATE into the evening. Afterward, she remained at her computer working for another couple of hours. Marcus stepped in carrying a plate of mushroom chicken, rice, and string beans. He didn't interrupt her. He set the plate on the desk beside her and walked out without saying a word. She didn't realize how hungry she was until she began eating. She planned to take a few bites as she worked, but one bite wasn't enough. She pushed her keyboard aside and didn't get back to it until the plate held only chicken bones and smears or mushroom gravy. She finished working around nine-thirty.

Marcus sat in the living room alone watching CNN when she finally emerged from being stuck in front of her computer. Ansinette laid down with her head in his lap. She muttered, "It seems like I work more from home. I can't wait for this lockdown to be over, so I can go back to work."

Marcus didn't reply. She followed his eyes to the television. The news report explained how many state governors were extending their stay-at-home measures across the country.

Coronavirus deaths had risen above fifty thousand. Images of eighteen wheelers with bodies stacked inside the trailers horrified Ansinette. It felt like they were living in what old people in her church used to call the last days. Pandemonium. Food shortages. Disease. Death. The stable world she had grown up in had changed in a matter of weeks.

She looked at Marcus. His hands curled into the soft tuft of her hair. She said. "Looks like we'll be locked in for another couple of weeks, huh?"

Marcus' lips pursed in a flat line of worry. "Looks like it."

Ansinette sat up. "What's wrong?"

"I'm tired of the way the government is handling things. We've got a president who wants to tell everybody to stay at home one day, then tells protesters that they're right for wanting the lockdown to be over. This whole thing makes no sense. They give a fraction of the stimulus package to us—the people who need it most—while corporations that don't need the money get the lion's share. It's the little people who have to pay back their money, while the big corporations don't. They get up there in Washington and think only of themselves and their pockets. That's it. We live in an unjust world that gets worse every day."

Ansinette watched him. "I didn't know you felt so . . . "

"And how do they expect us to survive if we can't go

back to work? The government isn't going to keep giving out checks."

"What's the alternative?" she asked him. "Let everybody go back to work so they can spread the virus and die?"

He sat silently contemplating. "I guess it doesn't matter what they do. We have to find a way to make it."

"We will," she added. "Together."

He said, "You don't understand how corrupt the government is."

Ansinette leaned over and kissed him. He kissed her back, but without his usual passion. She rested her head on his chest and listened to his heartbeat while stroking his forearm. The lockdown hadn't been easy for anyone. They were all a little stir crazy, but at least they had each other. She couldn't imagine being locked in a house with anyone else. She wouldn't want to be.

Although Ansinette understood Marcus' frustration, she didn't understand the source for his anger toward the government. She lay there quietly waiting for his fury to subside when he blurted, "My mother called me in a panic. She told me that my brother had been arguing with his girlfriend and she didn't know what he was going to do."

Ansinette sat up again. Marcus stared straight ahead, his eyes focused not on the television or the wall, but on some distant memory that only he could see. "Baby," she said. "What are you talking about?"

Marcus ignored the question. "I was living off campus by then. I had a little apartment with some friends. Louisiana was a long way away from North Carolina, but I had to do something. My mom didn't want to call the police because they would arrest my brother. She had no one else to call. I drove so fast that I made it here in nine hours. It usually took thirteen."

Ansinette listened intently as he spoke, lost as to what he was speaking about. She decided not to interrupt him.

"Michael shared a house with some friends we grew up with–well, they let him live there. He never worked a day in his life. I don't know how he survived. He was twenty-five damn near homeless, and out of his mind. He'd been with this white girl named Becca since high school. My mother had always told me that Michael was abusive toward Becca, but I had never witnessed it myself. All of that changed, though.

"He had Becca locked in his bedroom when I got there. I didn't know exactly what he had done to her, but Michael was not pleased to have me asking questions. All of his roommates were sitting around drinking and smoking weed. They didn't mention Becca or acknowledge that she had been there. I tried to talk to Michael. He was bigger than me– had been whupping me since we were little–and I respected him.

"But I could hear Becca crying through his bedroom door, and I knew something wasn't right. I asked Michael if I could see her. He said that she had been trying to leave him, and she couldn't see anyone until she changed her mind. I tried to go into the room. He punched me in the face. I yelled to his roommates to help me, but they sat there watching. I fought him hack. By then I had been lifting weights for football, and he couldn't handle me. I threw him through his bedroom door. Becca was curled up in a corner of the room. Both of her eyes were black and swollen. She hurried past us while we were going at it. We were still fighting when the police showed up."

Ansinette's gaze traced a single tear as it slid down Marcus' cheek. She wanted to reach out and wipe it away, but she reasoned that he needed that tear to wash away the remnants of a pain that had held him down for too long.

"I didn't know why they arrested me. I told them that I drove out there to help Becca, but they wouldn't listen. They handcuffed everyone in the house. They pushed me past a squad car where Becca sat crying in the backseat. I shouted for her to tell them I was innocent. All she had to do was tell them the truth. She turned her head and pretended not to hear me. They shoved me into the back of a cop car. I didn't find out that Becca told the cops Michael and I had raped and threatened to kill her until they had me in the interrogation room. They had taken statements from Michael's roommates corroborating Becca's story."

Ansinette felt her heart pounding wildly in her chest. She couldn't believe he had lived through such an ordeal. She reached out to stroke his thigh, reminding him through touch that he wasn't alone.

He said, "I remember seeing news stories about wrongfully convicted people serving decades of their lives in prison. I never knew how real it was. But when you're going through it, you see just how screwed up the justice system and government are."

She thought back to his anger about how the federal government was handling the pandemic. She had assumed his anger originated from the present situation. Now, she knew that his anger was born from the injustice he experienced. Marcus had been destroyed by the government in the worst way possible—destroyed in ways no one would ever truly understand.

"The district attorney knew that I was innocent. They still tried to force me into a plea bargain. First thirty years, then fifteen. I wouldn't take them. Finally, they offered me probation if I agreed to testify against my brother. They convinced my public defender to tell me I would die in prison if I took it to trial. My mother begged me to take it. She knew that I hadn't done anything, but she had grown up during the civil rights era. She saw black men beaten by white cops for nothing. She was afraid that once they had me locked up, I would never get out."

Ansinette licked her lips. "But you didn't take the plea, did you?"

Marcus shook his head. "I wasn't going to admit to something I didn't do. And I still had faith in the justice system. I never thought a jury would convict me once all the evidence was on the table. I was so stupid."

"You weren't stupid," she said. "You were a proud black man who was willing to suffer for what you believed in."

"Oh, I suffered. My brother's roommates testified against me. Becca said she didn't remember exactly who had raped her, but she thought it was me. Michael testified and told the jury that he tried to stop me from hurting Becca."

Ansinette's eyes bulged out of their sockets. "Your brother testified against you?"

"Did he? They offered him a plea for fifteen years. He took it with a smile. Everybody lied. If his roommates had admitted that they knew he was hurting Becca, they would have been just as guilty as him. Becca was scared to recant her story. Michael wanted to avoid a longer sentence. The whole situation was a mess."

Ansinette took his hand in hers. "Did you testify on your own behalf?"

"Of course. I didn't have anything to hide. I told the truth. One of my roommates from LSU testified as to when I left the apartment. My mother testified and backed up everything I said. They still convicted me."

Ansinette stared in her lap while shaking her head. "That's crazy."

"The judge sentenced me to sixty-three years in all. It was my first offense, but he hit me with the max for every charge."

Ansinette wondered how many nights he lay awake in bed, thinking about how his life should have turned out. Instead, he had been betrayed by friends and even his own family. She could not recall hearing of a worse tragedy. "How did you get out? They sentenced you to sixty years."

Marcus took a deep breath. "Becca's mom wrote me a letter explaining how Becca confessed to her about lying. She wasn't sure what to do with the information. I wrote back and told her to contact a lawyer. She convinced Becca to tell the truth."

Ansinette smiled at the seemingly happy ending. "It was that easy, huh?"

"Not at all. Becca's mom found an attorney willing to take the case for free, but the state fought me every step of the way. They pointed to Michael's testimony and those of his roommates. During my original trial prosecutors painted Becca as a fallen angel who had been disgraced by her abusive, black boyfriend. They brought her high school report cards that displayed straight A's. They showed videos of her singing in the church choir. But the second time around, when she was telling the truth, they pulled out her mugshots for minor drug possession and prostitution. They said that she was a career criminal and liar that shouldn't be trusted, except for when she had testified that I raped her." Marcus paused in thought. "Prosecutors are the best storytellers, but the truth is never their narrative."

Ansinette itched to hear the rest of the story. "But you got out?"

"I did. No fancy tricks, no lies. Becca stuck with the truth."

"Finally."

"Finally," Marcus admitted. "The state called Michael's roommates, they told the truth too. They admitted that they had only testified against me to keep themselves out of trouble. Michael refused to come to court. He wouldn't make a statement at all."

Ansinette couldn't understand how a brother could treat his family so wrong. She would never betray Robin in that way. There were times when she would have died for her sister. Blood was a bond that should never be broken. She wanted to ask if he had spoken to his brother since his release, but she thought that she already knew the answer.

Marcus' facial features softened noticeably. Ansinette moved closer to hold him. Marcus rested his face against her breasts. He did not tremble. He did not weep. She hoped that the one tear he shed earlier would be the last.

"Thank you for telling me," she said.

"Thank you for allowing me to tell you in my own time."

Ansinette kissed him then, wishing to express her sympathy. She took him by the hand and led him to their bedroom.

Fifteen

MARCUS

THEY BOTH LAY AWAKE. It was early. How early, he didn't know. He refused to look at the clock. Ansinette snuggled closer in his arms. They were naked. Marcus' hand roamed the contours of her curvy body.

Just as he was rising to erection, his phone rang. He looked at the smartphone on the nightstand. "Who in the hell is calling me this early?" He picked up the phone but didn't answer it. The clock read seven-twenty. The phone number was one he didn't recognize. He laid the phone down.

Ansinette laughed. "Who is it?"

"I don't know. I don't care."

"Answer it."

"Why? So they can tell me that I won a free trip to

Zimbabwe? All I have to do is send them a Cash App for twenty-thousand dollars?"

"Marcus . . ."

He answered the phone.

A strange voice greeted him. "Good morning. Is this Mr. Marcus Jenkins?"

Marcus bolted upright in bed. "This is him."

"Great. Great. This is Bob Waller. I interviewed you for Panda Intelligent Ware a few weeks ago."

A smile spread across Marcus' face as he listened. "I remember, sir. How could I forget?"

Ansinette touched his arm. "Who is it?" she whispered.

Marcus shushed her silently then put his phone on speaker so that she could hear. Bob Waller continued, "I'm sorry to bother you so early, but I've been working from home during the lockdown, and my hours are off a bit."

"It's fine." Marcus told him. "I would have taken your call in the middle of the night."

"Well, Marcus, I've got to be honest with you. I've been looking over your resume, and when compared with the other candidates, the only thing you lack is experience. The others have worked as project managers before. You haven't."

Marcus felt his heart pick up pace. "Well, Mr. Waller, I've been a shift manager at my current job for—"

Mr. Waller cut him off. "There's a difference between managing a meat packing plant and a billion-dollar sect of a fortune five-hundred corporation."

Adrenaline surged in Marcus' veins. It was apparent that he wouldn't get the job. His lips drew into a tight line of frustration. *I can't do anything right*, he thought to himself.

I am destined to be a failure. He looked to Ansinette.

Her gaze softened. She pushed the phone down a bit and whispered, "Calm down, baby. He wouldn't be ringing your phone if he didn't want to hire you."

He decided to listen.

Mr. Waller said, "What stands out about you most is what would probably turn off a lot of other employers."

"What do you mean?"

"Well, I have done extensive research on your criminal history, Marcus. Most employers wouldn't hire a man who has been to prison, even if he was falsely accused. That stigma taints a person for the rest of their life. With you I see it differently. Your resilience projects your character. Look what you did after getting out. You got a job and finished school. Most ex-cons haven't made the strides you have in such a short time. Your ability to bounce back shows how you react to adversity and how you handle pressure. I like that about you. Human resources raised holy hell about me wanting to hire you, but I assured them that you'd be fine under my wing. I don't expect you to cause any trouble."

"No, sir," Marcus stated. "My days of trouble are over."

"Okay then. If you still want the job, you'll have to start by working from home. We don't know when this lockdown will end, and I need you to begin training now. If you don't have a laptop, I'll have one sent to you within the day."

"I have everything I need, Mr. Waller."

"Good. Good. Today is Wednesday; I'll email you all the tax and employment forms, complete them and send them back by Friday. You'll start training on Monday. I'll have someone Zoom with you for training."

"I'm ready, Mr. Waller."

Mr. Waller said his goodbyes, but before he could hang up. Ansinette mouthed the words. *How much money?*

"Mr. Waller."

"Yes, Marcus?"

"We didn't discuss my salary?"

The phone went quiet. Finally, Mr. Waller said, "I gave that a lot of thought. Because of your inexperience, I can't pay you top dollar. I have to start you at one-twenty. If your first six months goes well, I'll raise you to one-seventy-five. How does that sound?"

Ansinette's eyes bulged in their sockets.

When Marcus didn't respond to Mr. Waller's question, he said, "I can go up to one-thirty. I didn't think you would drive such a hard bargain. Is that enough?"

Ansinette nodded her head fiercely.

Marcus stuttered, "Um . . . one-thirty sounds great."

"Okay, it's settled then. I'll email you the information."

Marcus and Ansinette bounced up and down on the bed after hanging up with Mr. Waller. They giggled like school kids on the first day of summer. Marcus wrapped Ansinette up in a hug and kissed her. They fell back on the bed with him on top.

Ansinette giggled again. "You got the job!" She declared, "I knew you would!"

"I'm glad you did, because I didn't."

She kissed his nose. "You don't have to worry about it anymore. Things are going to be great for you." Ansinette smiled so brightly that Marcus didn't think she could stop if she wanted to. "You should be able to buy your house now. You make almost twice as much as I do."

Marcus laid down on her. "Our house."

She pulled back to look into his eyes. "Do you really want to live with me?" He nodded.

She said, "I stink in the morning. I fart. And don't feed me ice cream after midnight."

Marcus screwed up his face. "You gonna turn into a gremlin?"

She chomped her teeth. "Worse."

"I might as well get ahold on you now while it's safe." He grabbed her and worked his way between her legs.

Ansinette pulled the sheet over his backside.

He was seconds from entering her when the bedroom door burst open. Marcus hopped off of Ansinette shouting. "What the fuck?" He spotted two men wearing facemasks standing in the bedroom. After staring at them, he recognized Devon, Ansinette's ex, and Mr. Roper, the apartment complex manager. He was a white man with gray hair.

Ansinette snatched the sheet from Marcus and scrambled to cover herself.

He stood up unashamed of his nudity. "What are you doing here?" he asked both Devon and Mr. Roper.

Devon stared between Marcus' legs with awe in his eyes. "My God. It's so big."

Marcus knelt to grab a pair of pants.

Mr. Roper turned to Devon. "You told me that you suspected foul play!"

"Foul play?" Marcus spat while sliding on his pants. "What is he talking about, Mr. Roper?"

"I'm sorry, Mr. Jenkins," Mr. Roper said to Marcus. "But this man came to my office and claimed that he needed to get into this apartment because he feared his children were victims of violent foul play."

Ansinette stood, wrapped the sheet around her nakedness, and pointed to the door. "Get out of my apartment!"

Mr. Roper turned to Ansinette. "Now look here, ma'am, I'm sure this is all a big mistake."

Devon smirked. "You're damn right this is a mistake." He looked to Ansinette, "I told you what I would do if I found out you had this rapist living with my sons."

"Leave him alone, Devon," Ansinette commanded. "This is between you and me."

Marcus finished zipping his fly. He looked from Devon to Mr. Roper feeling blood boil in his veins.

Devon continued. "Tell it to the judge, Ansinette. I knew you were a whore when I first met you. I tried to make you a respectable woman. But look at you."

Marcus pointed at him. "Don't talk to her like that."

Devon stepped closer to Marcus. "And you. Who do you think you are, taking advantage of a good woman?"

Ansinette struggled to keep the sheet wrapped around her body as she shuffled closer.

"Devon, no one took advantage of me. I asked Marcus to stay with us."

"I'll bet," Devon replied. "After he gamed you. That's what criminals learn to do in prison."

"I asked him to stay with us because I love him, Devon. I love him more than I ever loved you. If you don't like it, don't give me any more money, don't pick up your sons. Leave us the hell alone. I don't care. But you won't storm in my house and tell me how to live my life."

Just then, they all turned to the door as little David asked, "What's going on in here?"

Anthony stood beside him. "Why are you guys yelling?"

Devon looked to his sons. "Boys, pack your bags. From now on, you'll be living with me."

Marcus inched closer to Devon. "Now, hold on a minute, you can't make that decision."

Anthony grabbed David and shook his head vehemently. "We're not going to live with you! We're staying with Marcus."

Devon recoiled as if he'd been slapped. "But I'm your father."

Anthony backed away. "You don't act like it." Both boys turned and went back into their bedroom. They closed and locked the door behind them.

Marcus stood staring at Devon and Mr. Roper with clenched fists and a heaving chest. He wanted to hurt Devon, but he knew that being rejected by his own children pained him in a way that Marcus never could. Ironically, Marcus wasn't satisfied by Anthony and David's actions. It was a sad ending to a bad relationship. Children should be able to depend on their father. They shouldn't have to turn their backs on him to shield themselves from the pain he caused.

Devon pushed Marcus in the chest. "This is your fault! You turned my kids against me." Ansinette tried to squeeze between them. "Devon, you need to leave."

Mr. Roper grabbed Devon by the arm. "Sir, you mislead me into entering this apartment.

It's time for us to leave. If you don't want to leave, I'll be forced to call the police."

"Call them," Devon said. "I am a Raleigh City Councilman. They can't touch me."

Mr. Roper threw his arms in the air. To Ansinette and Marcus, he said, "I'm sorry that we disturbed you this morning." He left the apartment.

"Devon, you might as well go with him," Ansinette added. "We don't have a thing to talk about."

"We do," he said. "I'm tired of you turning my sons against me."

Marcus stepped around Ansinette. "You did that to yourself. Don't blame her because you're a terrible father. Those boys need you, and you don't care about them. You're a sorry excuse for a man."

Without warning, Devon cocked back and swung on Marcus. The blow caught him square on the chin and barely caused Marcus to flinch. He'd been hit ten times as hard by three-hundred-pound defensive linemen. Marcus struck back before he could stop himself. He tried to punch a hole in the side of Devon's head. When Devon fell to the floor, Michael straddled him and tried to do it again. He beat him until his hands hurt and he had to hammer down with the sides of his fists instead of his knuckles. He heard nothing. He saw only Devon's head bouncing off the floor each time he struck him. He beat him until the police ran into the apartment and pulled him off.

The bloodlust pushed all emotion aside. Marcus forgot about his job, his truck, the life he had built, and his new family. In that moment of violence, none of that mattered. He didn't realize the severity of what he had done until he felt an officer plant a knee into his back to handcuff him. Sound came rushing back to his ears then. He heard Ansinette screaming for them to let him go.

An ambulance arrived as they were shoving Marcus into the back of a police squad car. The paramedics ran inside with a stretcher and brought Devon out seconds later. His face was a bloody mess, but he wasn't beaten too badly. The paramedics allowed Devon to sit on the bumper of the ambulance while they tended to his wounds. A police officer wrote down Devon's statement. Devon pointed to Marcus in the squad car, pantomiming like a mad lion had attacked him.

Marcus watched with sober eyes. He was going back to prison. In a way, he didn't care. It would be consistent with the course of his life. He had risen on a pedestal of happiness, only to be knocked down by reality enough times to recognize the signs. His only regret was feeling that he was dragging Ansinette down with him.

Ansinette bolted down the stairs barefoot in jeans and a T-shirt. She squinted into the squad car. Her eyes narrowed to slits when she spotted Marcus inside. "Let him go!" She shouted, "He was protecting me!" She pointed to Devon. "He broke into my apartment. Arrest him! He started the whole thing!"

A white cop walked over to subdue her. She snatched away when he attempted to grab her arms. The cop reached down and laid a hand on his holstered pistol. Ansinette wouldn't back down. She declared, "Oh, you gonna shoot me now?"

Mr. Roper pulled up in his car and got out to approach the officer accosting Ansinette. Marcus couldn't hear what he said, but he noticed the cop look his way, then to Devon as Mr. Roper explained what happened. Ansinette nodded her head furiously to accentuate Mr. Roper's version of the events.

After listening to Mr. Roper, the cop walked to the squad car and let Marcus out. While removing the handcuffs, he told Marcus. "I'm really sorry about all of this. I'll need a statement about what happened."

Marcus rubbed his sore wrists where the handcuffs had

bitten into them. "Don't worry about it." Marcus went to Ansinette, who wrapped him up in a hug.

The cop strode to Devon and slammed him face down on the ground. Devon hollered, "What are you doing?"

The cop responded, "Arresting you for unlawful entry and trespassing."

"Arrest?" Devon protested as he was jerked to his feet. "You can't arrest me! I'm a city councilman. I know people."

The cop smirked. "You'll have one phone call to contact them."

Marcus stood beside Ansinette as the squad car drove away with Devon in the back. He draped his arm across her shoulders and whispered. "I'm sorry that I overreacted."

Ansinette kissed his cheek. "He needed his ass whupped. I just didn't want you to go to jail. I can't live without you."

Epilogue

ANSINETTE

ANSINETTE PEERED OUT OF THE WINDOW into the parking lot. She'd been standing there for some time, watching as a few people climbed in their cars and drove off. She wondered how many people had jobs to go to. Most of the world had not reopened. The parking lot remained desolate for the most part, but she stared out of the window nonetheless, as she had on countless mornings. A gentle breeze blew in causing her skin to prickle beneath the thin robe she wore.

"Come back to bed," Marcus said to her.

She turned and saw him lying there, wearing only a smile and a twist of the sheet bunched over his naked body. She walked over and climbed to him on the bed. Her robe spilled open, revealing her nudity beneath. He sat up to kiss her. His hand stole into her robe and squeezed her soft breast. Soon after, the robe fell away and they lay side by side in bed. Ansinette kicked a leg over his waist as they kissed.

Last night, they had seen Devon's mugshot on the nightly news. The news showed footage of him hurrying from the jail house after bonding out. The Lexus he escaped to was driven by a chubby white woman with flaming red hair. His constituents were calling for his resignation. A month ago, Ansinette would have been pulling out her hair at the thought of not receiving a check from Devon. She never realized how much she depended on him until the threat of him abandoning her loomed on the horizon. Now, she couldn't care less.

Ansinette reached between her and Marcus to tuck him inside her. They had been making love daily. The couple could never get enough of each other. She wondered how long the intensity would last. She hoped forever. She had finally found the puzzle piece that completed the complicated picture of her life. And to think, they never would have hooked up if the Coronavirus had not taken the country by storm.

After Devon's news story, she and Marcus saw images of riots in California, deaths in New York, and much much confusion in Washington D.C. So many people called for an end to the lockdown because they wanted to go back to work. They needed money. They were tired of being forced into quarantine.

But as Marcus moved inside of Ansinette, she gripped him tighter, wishing to hold on to the short time they had together. With each passing day of the lockdown, she could only beg for another. Ansinette felt bad for the rest of the world, and she wished they could feel the way she felt.

THE VIRUS BROUGHT ME MY FIRST LOVE

Instead of boredom and isolation, she couldn't believe that the virus brought her first love.

Best Sellers

WWW.WCLARKPUBLISHING.COM

W•CLARK PUBLISHING
A STATEMENT IN LITERATURE
WWW.WCLARKPUBLISHING.COM
WAHIDA CLARK
Best Sellers
WAHIDA CLARK
WHAT'S REALLY HOOD!
WAHIDA CLARK
THUGS AND THE WOMEN WHO LOVE THEM
WAHIDA CLARK
WAHIDA CLARK PRESENTS
LICKIN' LICENSE II
INTELLIGENT ALLAH
FLO ANTHONY
WAHIDA CLARK PRESENTS
LICKIN' LICENSE
INTELLIGENT ALLAH
WAHIDA CLARK PRESENTS
SERENITI HALL
WAHIDA CLARK PRESENTS
MY GUIDE TO LOVE & ROMANCE
WAHIDA CLARK PRESENTS
SECRET
SPARKLE
SAVAGE
WAHIDA CLARK PRESENTS
SERENITI HALL
SWAG
ANGEL SANTOS
SWIPE
KAYENNE
WAHIDA CLARK PRESENTS
THIRSTY
KARMA
TASH HAWTHORNE
IN STORE NOW
W. Clark Distribution & Media Corp.

CPSIA information can be obtained
at www.ICGtesting.com
Printed in the USA
LVHW110858260821
696094LV00003B/62